**Seth scooped his son up
and held him against his chest.
"Davy, say hello to Ms. White."**

Davy stuck his finger in his mouth, then apparently decided she was okay and lunged toward her. Julie's arms went out automatically to g his arms around h

"Sorry about that.

"That's all right."
"Hello, Davy. It's nice to meet you.

The words were conventional. Her expression wasn't, and it rocked him back on his heels.

He took a breath, trying to adjust his impressions of her once again. His brother wouldn't call her an ice maiden now. Julie had plenty of feelings.

The rest of that conversation flickered through his mind. No, he certainly wouldn't be expressing any interest in Julie White. He wanted someone safe, and what he read in Julie's sea-green eyes wasn't safe at all.

Books by Marta Perry

Love Inspired

MARTA PERRY

has written everything from Sunday school curriculum to travel articles to magazine stories in twenty years of writing, but she feels she's found her home in the stories she writes for Love Inspired.

Marta lives in rural Pennsylvania, but she and her husband spend part of each year at their second home in South Carolina. When she's not writing, she's probably visiting her children and her beautiful grandchildren, traveling or relaxing with a good book.

Marta loves hearing from readers and she'll write back with a signed bookplate or bookmark. Write to her c/o Steeple Hill Books, 233 Broadway, Suite 1001, New York, NY 10279, e-mail her at marta@martaperry.com, or visit her on the Web at www.martaperry.com.

HERO DAD

MARTA PERRY

Steeple
Hill®

Published by Steeple Hill Books™

STEEPLE HILL BOOKS

Steeple
Hill®

ISBN 0-373-87306-9

HERO DAD

www.SteepleHill.com

Printed in U.S.A.

For God has not given us a spirit of fear,
but of power, and of love, and of a sound mind.
—*2 Timothy* 1:7

This story is dedicated to Herb and Barb Johnson,
with much love.
And, as always, to Brian.

Chapter One

She was not afraid. Julie Alexander paused in front of the trim brick firehouse, clutching her camera bag as if it were a lifeline. She wasn't afraid to go inside and risk confronting the man who had the power to break her heart.

No. The denial was instant and automatic. She didn't have to risk anything. As long as Seth Flanagan didn't know who she was, she had nothing to fear.

For God has not given us a spirit of fear— The promise ought to be familiar to her. She'd had to rely on it often enough.

The red brick of the building in front of her looked mellow in the late September sunshine, like so many of the century-old brick buildings she'd seen in this small Pennsylvania city. The bay doors stood open, revealing the red and chrome hoods of fire engines. As she moved, an orangey red leaf from one of the maples that lined the street fluttered past her shoulder. It clung for a moment to the camera bag and then dropped at her feet. Her mind automatically began to compose a picture.

But there would be no hiding behind the camera lens today, no matter how much she might wish it. She stepped over the leaf and into the cavernous interior of the firehouse.

Three men leaned against a fire truck, their strong bodies forming a frame around the gold letters on its side: Suffolk Fire Department. She picked out Seth Flanagan instantly from the photograph her private investigator had provided.

His face, relaxed and smiling, was turned toward one of the other men, who was obviously telling a story. They hadn't seen her yet, which gave her a moment to study him. He was tall, solidly built, with broad shoulders and deep auburn hair that might once have been red. That easy grin of his had probably been the first thing that had attracted her sister.

Though she hadn't moved, something alerted the men to her presence. Seth straightened, frowning a little as his gaze met hers. He started toward her.

Her heart jolted at that frown. If he knew who she was—

No, he couldn't know. Lisa had been very clear, in that last letter of hers, that her two lives would never touch in any way. Her husband and his family would replace the birth family that had made her so unhappy.

She arranged a smile and stepped toward him. "Hello. I'm looking for Seth Flanagan."

Julie Alexander might know what her brother-in-law looked like, but photojournalist J. White certainly shouldn't.

"I'm Seth." He held out his hand, but the frown lingered in eyes that were so bright a golden brown that they looked like topaz. "You'd be the photographer. The chief told us you were coming."

The way he said the words revealed the reason for the frown. It wasn't her personally he objected to. It was being expected to work with her.

"I'm very grateful to Chief Donovan for his cooperation." She chose her words carefully. She'd better make it clear that his cooperation wasn't optional. "He's told me that your family will be perfect for my photo article on firefighters."

"You wanted a family of firefighters, and that's us." One of the other men approached.

Hair so dark it was almost black, eyes a deep Irish blue, as tall as Seth but not as broad—the coloring might be different, but the resemblance was still strong enough that she'd have pegged them for brothers even if she hadn't known.

"And you are?" She held out her hand.

"Ryan Flanagan." The smile he turned on her probably charmed every woman he met. "I'm the one the chief should have assigned to work with you."

She disengaged her hand. "I'm sure he had reasons for his choice." Aside from the fact that she'd manipulated her requirements to be sure he picked Seth.

"Yeah. He's grooming my big brother for promotion." Ryan elbowed Seth and got a glare in return. "Thinks he's got what it takes to move up."

Some emotion she couldn't identify flickered across Seth's face for a second, and then it was gone. "The chief just knows I'm more reliable than you are, that's all."

"But less fun." Ryan turned the grin on her again. "So, J. White. What does the J. stand for?"

"Julie."

"Pretty name."

She glanced at Seth, to find him watching his brother's flirting, a slight smile on his face. At a guess, that was a habitual posture for him, standing back, watching his brother show off. He didn't seem to need to be the center of attention. Solid, masculine, he was a man used to tough work and comfortable in his own skin.

"Enough, Ryan." He brushed his brother off easily when he was ready. "This is business, not romance central. Go polish a truck."

The man behind them snickered. Ryan shot a look toward him and then shrugged. "Later, Julie." He gave her that charming smile once more and moved off.

"The chief says it'll take a couple of weeks for you to do this article of yours." Seth's reluctance came through in the words. "That seems like a long time to be tagging around after us."

"You make me sound like a little sister who wants to play with the big boys."

His grin appeared again, relaxing his face. "I already have one of those, thanks. She's a paramedic with the department. Believe me, she outplays the big boys."

That would be Terry, she knew from the private investigator's report. "I'd like to meet her."

"You will if you're really doing this story on us."

Again she sensed his unwillingness. She'd better try to establish some sort of rapport with him if she wanted to get close enough for this to work.

"I know it sounds as if my presence is going to be an imposition, but I promise, eventually you'll forget I'm even there. That's when I'll get the pictures that will tell the story."

"A family of firefighters. I know." He said the words with a certain air of resignation, as if he were used to being categorized that way.

"It'll be a good story." Assuming she actually published it. For an instant she felt confused. This was the first time in her professional life that the story was just an excuse for another objective.

"Well, the family has agreed, so I guess we're in, but maybe you'd better meet us before you decide whether we're right for your project. My mother asked me to invite you to the house for supper tonight. Everyone won't be there, but enough of us."

He's from a big family, Lisa's letter had said. All noisy and in each other's faces all the time. At first it drove me crazy, but now I love it.

Lisa hadn't needed to point out how different it was from the Alexander family. She'd known Julie would understand.

"That sounds great." Seth couldn't know that she was cringing inwardly at the idea of meeting the Flanagans en masse.

"Around six, okay? We eat early so my little boy can have supper with us."

Davy would be there. Her heart began to thump. She would see her sister's child.

"Six is fine."

Seth patted the pockets of his uniform pants. "Do you have something I can write the address on?"

She pulled a notebook and pen from her bag. He bent closer, his head near hers as he scribbled an address in the book. She got a faint whiff of soap, saw the sprinkling of freckles on his skin, felt the sheer masculine magnetism of the man.

Okay. She tried to settle her jangling nerves. This first encounter was almost over and nothing bad had happened. The next one would be easier.

She closed the notebook on the address and took a step back. "I'll see you at six, then."

She turned toward the door. Relief settled over her. She could escape.

"Julie?" Seth's voice held a question, and she glanced back at him. "Have we met before?"

A sudden panic rippled along her nerves. "No." It took an effort not to let the fear show in her voice. "I'm sure we haven't."

He shrugged. "You looked a little familiar to me when you smiled."

"Maybe I remind you of someone you know." Not Lisa. She and Lisa had had different mothers, and no one had ever thought they looked at all alike. Until Seth looked at her and saw something.

"That must be it." A phone rang somewhere behind Seth, and he turned toward the sound.

"I'll see you later," she said quickly, and fled to the door.

She didn't breathe again until she was safely out on the sidewalk. Of all the missteps she'd envisioned, she hadn't thought of this one.

What else hadn't she thought of? She slid into the car she'd rented for the trip, mind whirling. Had she missed anything else that could give her identity away to Seth? Or, worse, anything that could betray Lisa's secret to her father?

She gripped the wheel with both hands. *Help me, Lord. I'm walking a tightrope, and if I fall, an innocent child could pay the price.*

"All I'm saying is that she's not what I expected." Seth lowered the evening newspaper to frown at his brother. He'd put the paper up as a defense against Ryan's insistence on talking about Julie White, but it wasn't working.

Ryan picked up a couple of scattered magazines and stuffed them into the basket beside Mom's rocking chair. She'd whirled in from the kitchen a moment ago, taken one look at the two of them, and issued cleanup orders.

"How different?" Ryan grinned. "Prettier?"

"Maybe. I pictured a nosy battle-ax out to make us look stupid. Or a bleeding heart who'd write a tear-jerker that we could never live down."

Julie White hadn't fit either stereotype. With her cool, detached manner and her delicate blond looks, she had upset his calculations on how to deal with her. He stifled an exasperated sigh. He had enough to do without babysitting the woman through this story she wanted to do.

"She's no battle-ax, that's for sure." Ryan dropped into the chair opposite him.

Seth lifted an eyebrow at his younger brother. "Are you planning on asking her out?" Ryan had turned into the playboy of the family in recent years, never sticking with one woman for more than a few dates.

"I thought about it." Ryan shrugged. "But she's not really my type."

"*You* have a type? I thought you flirted with every female you met."

Ryan grinned and tossed one of the magazines at him. "I like a little warmth. J. White's a tad too cool and unfeeling for me. Ice maidens aren't worth the effort."

Seth considered that. He wouldn't have said *unfeeling* exactly. His sense of the woman had been that she was keeping a strong clamp on her emotions.

Ryan tossed another magazine, always ready to

irritate one of his brothers. "So, why don't you ask her out? You're the one who's ready to get married, not me."

For the hundredth time Seth regretted confiding that in Ryan, of all people. "I didn't say I was ready to get married. Just that maybe I should think about it, for Davy's sake."

An almost-three-year-old needed a mother, and it wasn't fair to expect Mom to play that role indefinitely. So he had started looking around for someone who'd make a good mother, someone who wanted a marriage based on companionship and building a family together.

Not one based on romance. His mind veered away from thinking about Lisa. About how he'd failed her.

He was almost grateful for the knock on the door. "Behave yourself tonight." He frowned at Ryan, who grinned back, unrepentant. "And put those magazines away before Mom comes back in."

Ryan scooped the magazines from the floor and headed toward the kitchen. "I'll tell Mom she's here."

Some things hadn't changed since they were kids. Ryan still baited him, and he still let it happen. Maybe he didn't bother trying to change things because teasing aside, he knew Ry would go to the wall for him.

He opened the door. Julie White clutched her camera bag tightly and gave him a polite smile.

"I hope I'm not too early."

"Just right." He gestured toward the living room. "Please, come in."

Why had she brought the camera bag with her to-night? Did she expect to start photographing them already? The thought still made him vaguely uneasy. They'd be baring their private lives to the woman, with no idea of her agenda or that she even knew what she was doing.

"Thanks." She stepped inside and paused next to him, as if not sure what to do next.

Her head barely made it to his shoulder. He hadn't realized, when they'd talked at the station, how small she was. Her light blond hair and pale ivory skin made her look as delicate as a porcelain doll.

An illusion, no doubt. No woman who'd talked the chief into agreeing to this story could be all that delicate.

She glanced up at him, soft layers of hair flowing against the shoulders of the coral sweater she wore. And what was he doing, noticing what the woman was wearing, anyway? This was business, not social. Ryan's ribbing had taken over his thoughts.

"Are you sure I'm not too early?"

The repeated question clarified things for him. Julie was putting on a good front, but nervousness lay behind it.

"Relax." He grinned, taking her arm. "We don't bite, honest."

Her face eased in a smile that melted whatever ice Ryan seemed to think was there. Seth blinked. That smile could thaw a glacier. Maybe he'd have to read-just his view of Julie.

"My nerves are showing, huh?"

"Well, you're gripping that camera bag as if you intend to attack someone with it."

She let go of the bag, shaking her fingers. "I'm always a little stressed when I'm starting a new project."

He nodded toward the bag. "Did you want to start taking pictures already?" He hoped not. Maybe, given a day or two, he'd get used to the idea of having a stranger recording their lives. Or maybe not.

"Not until your family is ready." Her smile took on a tinge of embarrassment. "I'm afraid the camera is my security blanket. If I don't have it with me, I always think I'll miss the best shot of my career."

"Somehow I doubt that dinner with the Flanagans will give you that."

"I also brought along a few magazines that contain some of my photo essays. I thought seeing them might reassure you that I know what I'm doing."

He must have been too obvious. "I'd love to see some of your work."

"So would I." His mother swept into the room and over to them, still moving as lightly as a girl in spite of having five grown children. Six, if you counted Brendan, the orphaned nephew she'd raised.

His mother grasped Julie's hand warmly in both of hers. "I'm Siobhan Flanagan. Welcome to our home. Goodness, Seth, what are you doing keeping Ms. White standing here like this? She'll think I didn't raise you right."

"Julie, please, not Ms. White," she said.

The words were right, but there was something strained about Julie's smile that told him nervousness had taken hold again. What was wrong with the woman? Nobody could be more warm and welcoming than Siobhan Flanagan.

"I'm sure she's not going to blame my shortcomings on you, Mom."

"You kids came by those all by yourselves, didn't you?" His mother swatted him lightly. "I don't know how I got through raising the lot of you."

He grabbed her and kissed her cheek. "Go on, now. Which of us would you like to get rid of?"

He glanced toward Julie as he spoke, and her expression startled him. For pity's sake, she looked as if she'd never seen horseplay before. If that was the case, she wouldn't last around the family long enough to do that story of hers.

His mother seemed to notice something, as well. She freed herself from his grasp, probably intending to try and put Julie at ease. But whatever she might have said was lost in the thunder of running feet.

Davy charged in from the kitchen at the headlong run that was his preferred method of locomotion. "Daddy, Daddy, Daddy." The yell was earsplitting. "I help Grammy make supper."

"I'll bet you did, Davy-boy." He scooped his son up and tossed him in the air, then held him against his chest. "Davy, say hello to Ms. White."

Davy stuck his finger in his mouth, afflicted with

sudden shyness, then apparently decided she was okay and lunged toward her. Julie's arms went out automatically to grasp him, and he threw his arms around her neck in a hug.

She looked a little stunned.

"Sorry about that. Davy's a born hugger."

"That's all right." Her voice was muffled as she returned his son's embrace. She pulled back a little. "Hello, Davy. It's nice to meet you."

The words were conventional. Her expression wasn't, and it rocked him back on his heels.

He took a breath, trying to adjust his impressions of her once again. Ryan wouldn't call her an ice maiden if he saw the way she looked now. Julie had plenty of feelings.

The rest of that conversation flickered through his mind. No, he certainly wouldn't be expressing any interest in Julie White. He wanted someone safe, and whatever he was reading in Julie's sea-green eyes wasn't safe at all.

Julie felt as if she'd taken a blow to the heart. She was too overwhelmed with feelings to think straight, and she could only hope none of them showed on her face.

She'd told herself, objectively, that her mission here was clear. She had to make sure Lisa's child had the best, and then she'd step back out of his life again.

But she hadn't thought about how it would feel to hold a living, breathing, sturdy little boy in her arms. A squirming little boy, she realized.

She set him down, thankful that the movement hid her face for a moment. When she stood again, she was composed.

"So this is your son. He's adorable."

He was. She didn't want to stop looking at him. He had a mop of soft red curls that glinted gold where the light touched. His eyes were the same golden brown that Seth's were, and he had a sprinkling of freckles across his cheeks.

"Yeah, we think he's a pretty neat kid." Seth's words were casual, but love and pride blazed across his face.

This was something else she'd left out of her planning. She hadn't imagined the power of the love Seth had for his child, and it left her groping for solid ground.

Davy ran across the room to his uncle. Ryan scooped him up and tossed him in the air, the boy's head nearly touching the ceiling. She flinched at the sight; they ought to be more careful with Lisa's child.

Davy might look like his father, but there was an indefinable something in his heart-shaped face that reminded her of Lisa. Her fingers itched to pull out her camera and start snapping.

"Did you say you had some articles to show us?" Siobhan Flanagan's question brought her back to her senses.

She couldn't start taking pictures of Davy. She couldn't do anything that would alert the Flanagan family to her interest in him.

"Yes, of course." She pulled several magazine issues from her satchel. "These should give you an idea of the type of piece I have in mind."

"Come, sit down." Siobhan took one of the magazines and handed another to Seth. Then she drew Julie down beside her on the well-worn sofa.

Julie began explaining the photo piece she'd done on women pilots, but she could only give it half of her attention. The other half was focused on Seth, who sat opposite them with an article she'd done on one of the grand old resort hotels of the Maryland shore. He frowned at something, and her throat tightened.

Ridiculous, to care what he thought of her work. They had no relationship, in spite of the fact that he'd been married to her sister. That was the way Lisa had wanted it. The way she wanted it.

He glanced at her. "I've seen this place, but your pictures make me think I've never really looked at it."

She was irrationally pleased. "I hope that's a compliment."

"It is."

He gave her that easy grin, and her breath caught. Seth might be the quieter of the Flanagans, but he packed a powerful masculine punch, all the same.

"I'm telling you, if we'd taken in a bigger line to begin with—"

Two men came in, their conversation stopping when they saw her. Even as she tried to identify them from what the investigator had told her, a young woman came in behind them, running her hand through tumbled red curls. More Flanagans, obviously.

Her nerves twitched again as Davy ran to the older man, who picked him up, kissed him, then tossed him casually to the woman. She'd be the first one to admit she didn't know anything about raising an almost-three-year-old, but surely all that stimulation couldn't be good for him right before supper.

She and Lisa had always had an early supper in the nursery, followed by bath and bed, supervised by a revolving progression of nannies and au pairs. She had a vague memory of Lisa's mother popping in to say good-night once they were in bed. She'd worn silk and diamonds and smelled of expensive perfume.

No one had stayed in their lives long. Not her mother or Lisa's mother or any of the nannies. She wouldn't want that for Davy, obviously, but was this better?

Her head already throbbed from too many people talking at once. There were way too many Flanagans.

She stood, trying to make sense of the introductions flying at her. Seth's father, Joe, bluff and hearty. His white hair still had traces of the red it had once been. Seth's minister cousin, Brendan, who was also the fire department chaplain, explained that his fiancée was working late so he'd come to beg supper from his aunt. The red-haired young woman was Terry, Seth's paramedic sister.

Too much confusion. She backed up until she bumped into the mantel. This was better. She could stay out of the mainstream and observe. If only she could put a camera in front of her face, she'd be fine.

Did they always all talk at once? And pass Davy

around in that casual manner? Apparently there had been a fire call after she'd left the station that afternoon, and they were engaged in an animated argument over the order in which equipment had been called in.

She took a steadying breath. This was her chance to observe, she reminded herself. She could see how they interacted with Davy and with each other.

Seth was the quiet one, she realized, but not for any lack of strength. He came across as solid and even-tempered, a peacemaker in the face of some flippant remark of Ryan's that brought a rebuke from his father, or Terry's passionate defense to Brendan of some action Julie didn't understand. For that matter, they all seemed to be speaking a language they understood and she didn't.

In the midst of the hubbub, Seth's gaze met hers. His smile seemed to pierce her heart, adding another layer to the confusion.

He took a few steps toward her. "Still sure you want to have anything to do with the Flanagans?" he asked. "Trust me, it's even worse when the rest of the family is here."

Family. The word lodged in her mind like a shard of glass. What was she doing, trying to evaluate the family Lisa had chosen? She certainly didn't have any basis for comparison.

She could back out. It wasn't too late. She could leave, and no one would ever know.

Davy, racing across the room after a ball, ran full tilt into her. She stooped to catch him, seeing the laughter that lit his eyes and engaged his whole body.

Her breath caught, and for an instant she thought her heart did, too. Who was she trying to kid? She couldn't back out. For better or worse, she had to go through with this.

Chapter Two

Her mind fogged from a mostly sleepless night, Julie drove along the tree-lined street that led to the fire station. Even several cups of coffee had not been enough to clear her head. She wasn't ready to join Seth for this orientation meeting he'd arranged at the firehouse this morning, but she didn't have a choice.

She'd spent most of the night trying to sort out her feelings, only to find that they defied classification. She'd thought she could do this thing calmly, coolly, without emotional involvement. Instead she'd found that just seeing Davy had brought on a torrent of memories that hadn't surfaced in years.

One still clung, as insubstantial as a cobweb but just as hard to get rid of. Lisa couldn't have been much older than Davy, so Julie had probably been about five. Lisa had woken with one of the nightmares she'd had so frequently. Their nanny-of-the-moment hadn't been patient with children who cried after they'd been put to bed, so Julie had taken Lisa into bed with her.

They'd snuggled together, and she'd patted Lisa, telling her over and over that everything was all right. Finally she'd felt the small body relax into sleep against her.

It's all right, Lisa. I'll take care of you.

But she hadn't. If she had, maybe Lisa wouldn't have found it necessary to break all ties with her in order to start her new life.

I let her down. I didn't mean to, but I did. Did God accept that as an excuse? Probably not.

I won't let Davy down. I promise. I'll do what's best for Lisa's son.

That meant gaining Seth's acceptance in order to see what Davy's life was like, so that's what she would do.

Then what? For an instant something in her rebelled in answer to that. She'd have to disappear. She couldn't continue to be a part of Davy's life, because if she did, her father might find out that the boy existed.

Ronald Alexander's potential response to that knowledge was incalculable, but the only thing he'd ever loved was wielding power. If he knew about Lisa's child, he wouldn't be able to resist trying to control the little boy's life.

So he could never know. She drew up at the curb, switching off the ignition. She didn't have any choice but to go forward. Maybe, belatedly, she could keep the promise she'd made to Lisa.

She walked into the huge, echoing garage. Seth knew she was coming, so he'd be around someplace. A figure moved on the back of one of the fire trucks, drawing her attention. Seth jumped lightly to the concrete floor and came toward her.

"Julie. Hi."

He wiped his hands on a rag as he approached her, his body compact and sturdy in the uniform's dark blue pants and shirt with the red-and-white Suffolk Fire Department patch. Her stomach gave a little flutter of nerves.

"Hi. I hope this is a convenient time for me to pester you on the job."

"It's fine unless the alarm goes, but nobody can predict that." If he thought her presence was a nuisance, he must be determined not to let it show.

"Are you busy?" She nodded toward the cloth.

He grinned, tossing it aside. "Not really. It's just a compulsion firefighters have, to make sure their rigs look the best. If you see a sloppy or dirty apparatus, you don't think much of the firefighters who man her."

She filed that tidbit of information away for the article, assuming it got written. "I don't want to get in the way."

"A pretty visitor is never in the way." A wheeled platform rolled out from under the nearest truck, and the firefighter she'd seen the day before smiled up at her. "I'm Dave Hanratty."

"Married. With kids," Seth added.

"Hey, I'm married, not blind." Dave got up. "I can give Julie the tour if you're too busy."

She'd prefer that both of them stopped paying so much attention to her. "Really, I don't want to take either of you away from your work. If you'll just give me permission to start snapping, I'll disappear into the woodwork."

"You can take any pictures you want," Seth said. "But I'll show you around so you know what's where. Dave can go back to inspecting the undercarriage."

"Single guys get all the breaks," Dave complained. He pulled the platform over with his foot. "When you're ready for my close-up, just let me know."

"Who would want a close-up of that mug?" Seth asked innocently.

She was beginning to catch on to the ribbing that flowed ceaselessly between the men. "I promise," Julie said. "If I want a close-up, you'll be the first to know."

Laughing, Dave rolled himself smoothly back under the truck.

Seth gestured. "The engine room, but I guess you figured that out for yourself. We spend a lot of time here, cleaning, training, doing maintenance. Come on upstairs and see the rest of it."

She pulled out one of the cameras she'd brought with her. Chances were good that anything she shot today would look too stiff, but she had to start or they'd never reach the point of comfort.

Seth gave a sidelong look at the camera as he led

the way to the stairwell. She didn't have much trouble interpreting that look.

"The camera bothers you, doesn't it?"

He shrugged. "I guess. Who knows—you might catch me doing something I shouldn't, and then the chief would be on my back. Or something dangerous, and then my mother would be after me. Trust me, that's worse."

"What would you do that you shouldn't?

"Horseplay." He grinned. "Firefighters are great ones for practical jokes. Officially, the chief disapproves."

He stood back to let her go up the narrow flight of wooden stairs first. She could feel him behind her as she climbed. "I'd think your mother would be used to having firefighters in the family by this time."

"I guess mothers never stop worrying."

She paused at the top of the steps so she could see his expression. "What about you? It must worry you, being in a dangerous job when you're a single parent."

She might as well not have bothered, because his expression didn't give one thing away.

"I don't take chances," he said shortly. "This is the kitchen." He gestured. "We spend a lot of time here, and yes, we cook. People always ask that."

It was only as Lisa's sister that she really had the right to have asked that question about his job. He was a single father. He did have a potentially dangerous job. This would be so much easier if she could just tell him the truth.

Lisa hadn't wanted him to know about her family, either. That was the bottom line. She searched for a safe remark.

"Are you a good cook?"

His expression eased at the innocuous question. "My mother probably wouldn't think so, but I'm about as good as anyone else here. All of us here have to cook for the group occasionally. I make a mean chili, anyway."

She took a few shots of the kitchen that she'd undoubtedly delete from the digital camera, then continued snapping as he showed her a living area furnished with what looked like cast-offs from someone's house and a small exercise room furnished with weights and a punching bag.

He gestured toward a closed door. "Bunks and bathrooms are that way, but a couple of guys are sleeping right now."

"And if the alarm goes off?"

"If a call comes in, don't get between that door and the pole."

The shiny brass pole led through a hole in the floor to the engine room below. "So the pole really exists, does it?" She began snapping again. "I thought that might be a myth."

"There's a good reason for it. You have half a dozen firefighters trying to get down a flight of stairs at the same time, you got a mess. The pole's faster and safer."

She focused her lens on the opening. "You

wouldn't care to give me a demonstration, would you?"

"I will if you try it, too."

She studied him through her viewfinder. He looked serious. "I'm not the athletic type."

"If you're going to go out on calls with us, you'll have to stop hiding behind the camera and take a risk or two. And that's the whole idea of this, isn't it?"

The idea is to observe your relationship with my nephew.

"Sure, but that doesn't mean I want to become a firefighter."

"Come on." He grasped the pole with one hand and drew her forward, his eyes teasing. "Even the ten-year-olds in our Future Firefighters club slide the pole. I'll show you how. Just hang on here." He patted the shiny brass.

"I can't." She pulled back, feeling his arm strong around her. "You'd have to have three or four people down there to break my fall before I'd try."

He grinned. "The idea is to slide, not to fall."

"Even so—"

She looked up at his face, and her nerves gave that funny little jump again. He was too close—way too close. She could see the gold flecks in his brown eyes and the tiny lines that bracketed his firm mouth.

An inappropriate wave of warmth flooded her. Seth's eyes seemed to darken, as if he felt it, too.

Oh, no. She could not be attracted to Seth Flanagan. She couldn't be.

* * *

For just an instant Seth felt the way he had when a beam came down on him in a smoky fire. His helmet had protected him from serious injury, but he'd seen stars for a week afterward.

Looking into Julie's eyes seemed to create a similar effect. He let go of her carefully, putting some distance between them. He wasn't looking to see stars anymore, either physically or emotionally.

"Tell you what. I'll slide down to show you how it's done, but you can take the stairs. This time."

"Every time." Julie lifted the camera in front of her face. She did that a lot, maybe more than she had to. He couldn't help but wonder why she felt the need to hide.

"Okay." He went into his usual pole-sliding demonstration. "The alarm goes, you charge out, adrenaline pumping, and grab the pole with your arm, wrap your legs around and slide."

Julie's face disappeared as he slid down a little faster than usual. He landed hard enough to jolt him. Well, it served him right for showing off just because a pretty woman was watching.

He looked up at the opening, but she'd disappeared. He heard her footsteps on the stairs, and in a moment she emerged from the stairwell.

"Very impressive."

"Thank you. We try to keep up the image."

She nodded toward the closest rig. "Why don't you go back to the cleaning you were doing when I came in, and I'll just ask a few questions while I take a few more photos."

"Fair enough." At least cleaning would give him something to do with his hands. She seemed to think he was eventually going to forget that she and her camera were there, but he doubted that would ever happen.

He climbed up on the rig and looked down at her. "Seems like you're going to have to come up here, too, if we're going to talk." He held out his hand.

He could sense her hesitation. Then she nodded, grabbed his hand and let him pull her up onto the rig. She glanced around a little nervously.

"I'm not going to set off any sirens by touching the wrong thing, am I?"

"There's nothing you can hurt back here. The controls are in the cab." He grabbed a rag and started polishing the chrome strip. "Fire away."

He didn't forget she was there. But he did, oddly enough, begin to forget after a while that she was taking photographs. He polished the chrome, the familiar routine soothing. Julie had an easy, detached way of asking questions while she snapped that had him thinking about what he was saying instead of what she was doing.

"Does it bother Davy that you work such long shifts?"

His polishing slowed, and he turned to frown at her. Once again, he couldn't see her face because of the camera.

"Do you know that's the fourth question you've asked about my son? I thought this article was supposed to be about firefighting."

Julie held the camera in place a moment longer, but then she seemed to realize they weren't going any further until she answered. She lowered it, but her cool gaze didn't give anything away.

"The story is meant to be about a family of firefighters. Naturally I'm especially interested in the effects of that on the children."

"Then you should talk with my sister Mary Kate. She has two kids, and her husband's a firefighter."

"I plan to. But as a single father—well, you seem to have the more challenging role."

"I'm not so sure I want my private life included in your article."

Her expression grew a little cooler. "I need the contrast of work and family life. That's what the chief agreed to. That's what your family agreed to."

She had him there. They *had* all agreed, but he hadn't realized she intended to probe into *his* life in particular.

"I guess we did agree." He put the cloth down and leaned a little closer to her. He had the sense that she'd have backed up if there'd been any place to go. "Okay. I'll go along with that, but you have to do something for me in return."

She eyed him warily. "What?"

"I already mentioned it, but maybe you didn't realize I was serious. I want you to experience basic safety training. No matter what the chief says, I don't feel comfortable taking you to a fire scene unprepared."

She lifted her eyebrows, her green eyes as bright as a forest pond reflecting sunlight. "You wouldn't be trying to discourage me, by any chance, would you?"

"Certainly not." Well, not consciously, anyway. "I think it's important."

She shrugged. "Fine. I guess if I can go up in a fighter plane for my piece on women pilots, I can do this."

It sounded as if Julie was tougher than her delicate looks would indicate. "Okay. I'll put you through the basics until I'm satisfied you know how to handle yourself."

She leaned back against the side of the rig, studying him. "And in return, I get a chance to photograph you and Davy, right?"

He nodded. "You can start this afternoon, if you want. I'm scheduled to do a fire-safety presentation at Davy's nursery school. You can come along."

She looked a little startled. "Is he old enough for nursery school?"

"He turns three next week, so we started him for the fall session. He goes two afternoons a week, and he really loves it." He wasn't sure why he sounded defensive about it. He was Davy's parent, and it was up to him to decide if Davy was old enough for nursery school.

"Sorry, I didn't mean that as a criticism. I'm not around young children enough to know."

In that case, it was going to be interesting to watch the cool, detached photographer coping with a bunch of rug rats.

"Then maybe you'd better put on a safety helmet. And some earplugs. Because you'll be around plenty of them this afternoon."

The nursery school didn't really seem as noisy or intimidating as Seth had indicated when they approached it that afternoon.

"This isn't so bad." Julie scuffed through the fallen leaves as they walked across the lawn toward the building. Like so much of Suffolk, it was built of mellow old brick. "I don't hear a single scream."

"Just wait. You haven't encountered Davy's class of preschoolers yet." He hefted the large duffel bag that apparently contained the gear he needed for his presentation. "I went with them on a field trip to the pretzel factory earlier this month." He shuddered, grinning. "Not an event I care to repeat."

"It looks like a nice place." She was determined to be fair, in spite of her feeling that Davy was too young for nursery school. She nodded toward the bright play equipment scattered across the fenced yard under huge old oak trees.

"It's the best. Both of Mary Kate's kids went here." He hit a button next to the door, waved at the woman inside and then pulled the door open when the buzzer sounded. "Showtime," he said. "We're on."

"What do you mean, 'we'?" She followed him into

a hall decorated with murals and children's art work. "I'm just an observer."

"You find it safer that way, don't you?"

The remark startled her, but before she could find a response, he was opening a classroom door. She followed him in, wrestling with his comment, not sure whether to be insulted or not.

It wasn't a matter of playing it safe, she assured herself. Her profession required that she be a detached observer—that was all.

The children were seated at low round tables, apparently having a snack, but Davy jumped up at his father's entrance and raced to him for a hug. She watched his red-gold head nestled next to Seth's with an odd lump in her throat. Davy was her blood kin, too, but he'd probably never know that.

The teacher, a slender young black woman in jeans and a smock, clapped her hands. "All right, boys and girls. Davy's father is here to talk to us. Take your places on the rug, please."

Somewhat to Julie's surprise, the children did as the teacher directed, gathering in a ragged circle on the braided rug and wiggling like so many puppies as they sat.

She slipped to the side of the group, finding a spot where she'd be out of the children's line of sight. She sat down, pulling out her camera, automatically calculating the amount of light that poured through the large windows on the side wall.

"Some of you know that Davy's father is a firefighter," the teacher said. Davy grinned, obviously proud. "He's going to show us what to do if there's a fire."

Seth sat on the rug. If he was nervous about this presentation, it didn't show. "Hi, guys." He pointed to the patch on his uniform shirt. "Like Ms. Sarah said, I'm a firefighter. This patch says that I'm a member of the Suffolk Fire Department."

She focused the camera on his face, slipping into professional mode. Or maybe not so professional. She didn't usually dwell on a subject's easy grin, or the way the light made his eyes look almost gold instead of brown.

Stop it. So he's an attractive guy. That doesn't matter. All that matters is Davy's happiness.

She began taking pictures. A couple of the children glanced around at the first few clicks, but they soon forgot her. They were too engrossed in having a real live firefighter in their classroom.

That firefighter did a good job, she had to admit. He seemed to know just what would keep his young audience involved. No doubt because he had a child of his own, he didn't even miss a beat when one little boy began to wail that he had to go potty.

Not easily flustered, that was Seth. What would it take to ruffle that relaxed exterior? She couldn't guess. The calm, friendly manner seemed to be inherent in his personality. She could see why Lisa had been drawn to him.

He'd come well prepared, too, using stuffed toys of

familiar characters to illustrate fire safety. In his hands, a stuffed teddy bear stayed low and hurried out of a house of blocks.

"Remember, you never go back in, no matter what. Even if you left your favorite toy inside, don't go back in until a grown-up tells you it's okay. Right?"

They nodded solemnly.

"Okay, now we're going to practice what to do if your clothes should ever catch fire."

She blinked. Surely that was too scary for this young group.

Apparently Seth didn't think so. He demonstrated the stop-drop-and-roll routine himself, making them laugh. Then he had all the children practice. A lot of giggling punctuated the process.

She focused the camera on Davy, who was rolling vigorously, hands over his face. Would he pay for this in nightmares?

"Now, then." Seth regained their attention by dumping out the rest of the contents of his bag. "Ms. Julie is going to help me show you what a firefighter wears."

She frowned at him. "I don't think so."

He smiled back blandly. "I need a model. You're it."

The children, prompted by the teacher, started clapping. Apparently she didn't have a choice. She set the camera aside and joined him in front of the children.

"I'll get you back for this," she murmured.

"Promises, promises." He held out a pair of bulky yellow pants. "Ms. Julie is putting on the pants that will protect her at a fire. We call them bunker pants."

Easier said than done. She struggled into the pants, which fit surprisingly well. That meant he'd planned this, bringing an outfit from one of the female firefighters.

"Next come the boots."

She stuffed her feet into the boots, wondering how anyone managed to move in this outfit, let alone fight a fire. Seth fielded several comments from children who wanted him to know that they had boots, too.

"Now the bunker jacket." He held the yellow jacket, helping her to slip it on. He snapped the front of it as if she were a child, and then his fingers moved to the collar, tipping it up under her chin.

He looked at the children. "What else does Ms. Julie need to go to the fire?"

"The helmet," they chorused.

"Right you are." He settled the helmet on her head gently. His fingers brushed her cheeks as he fastened the chin strap.

Breathe, she reminded herself. Breathe.

For an instant she thought he skipped a beat. Then he went on smoothly. "Let's give Ms. Julie a hand for being such a good sport, okay?"

The children clapped again, making her ridiculously pleased, and then it was over. The teacher was leading them back to their tables, and Seth picked up the duffel bag.

He quirked an eyebrow, looking at her. "Need some help getting that off?"

"I can manage." She pulled off the helmet and ran

her fingers through her hair. "You planned that," she accused, keeping her voice soft.

"Hey, I don't usually have a model when I do this. You can't blame me for taking advantage of it."

"Can't I?"

He grinned. "You're a hard woman, Julie White. Come on, this wasn't so bad, was it?"

She helped him stuff the gear back into the duffel bag. "I guess not." She glanced toward the kids, who were joining the teacher in a song. Davy sang with gusto, his little arms waving in time to the music. "But don't you think that was scary for children this young?"

"Maybe so. But it's better than the alternative."

Something grim in his voice brought her gaze back to his face, and what she saw there startled her. The lines of his face had hardened. Only his eyes showed expression, and the emotion they betrayed was pain.

"You mean—" Her throat closed.

"We lost two children in an apartment fire the first year I was in the department." His words were flat, but not for any lack of emotion. If anything, Seth was feeling too much, not too little.

"I'm sorry," she whispered.

Their eyes met, and for an instant she felt as if she saw into his heart. She couldn't pull her gaze away. She was caught in the moment.

He shook his head, maybe shaking off the bad memories. "Well, anyway." He hefted the bag. "Are you getting what you want?"

For an instant the question confused her. Was she? Then she realized that Seth was talking about the shots.

"Yes, of course." She bent to pick up the camera bag, letting the action hide her face. Was she getting what she wanted? She wasn't sure she knew.

Chapter Three

"This is what you meant by taking me through some safety training?"

Julie watched Seth's face, hoping for a sign that he was kidding about this. She hadn't known what to expect when he'd picked her up at her hotel this morning, but it hadn't been this—a collection of thrown-together buildings on the outskirts of Suffolk, an expanse of asphalt and a hodge-podge of firefighting equipment.

"I know it doesn't look like much, but this is the Suffolk Fire Academy." He gestured at the fenced-in area. "Suffolk's big enough to have a professional fire department, but funding is always a problem."

"So they skimp on the academy?" It looked as much like a junkyard as anything else. She spotted a group of people in coveralls coming down the side of one of the buildings with ropes. Surely Seth didn't expect her to do that.

He grinned. "Firefighters don't expect luxury accommodations. Good thing, because they wouldn't get them."

Her journalistic mind began to kick in. "Surely the training is important enough to spend money on."

"Training, yes. Our recruits go through a tough twelve-week program. But there's never enough money to go around, and they can learn just as well in a Quonset hut as a fancy classroom."

One of the people descending the building had lost his or her grip and fallen the last few feet. She held her breath until the person was up again.

"You're not planning to have me do that, are you?" She nodded toward the group.

"Sadly, our insurance wouldn't cover that."

He was probably teasing again, but sometimes she found it difficult to tell. That constant teasing must be part of the firefighter culture. Or the Flanagan culture. They tended to blend.

"You get to meet another Flanagan." He nodded toward the man walking toward them, wearing the same blue uniform Seth did. A beautiful yellow Labrador walked at his side. "My brother Gabe."

"Hi, bro." Gabe slapped Seth's shoulder, and then extended his hand toward her. "You must be Julie. I'm sorry my wife and I couldn't make it to dinner the other night to meet you."

While she murmured pleasantries, Julie compared the two of them. Gabe was leaner than Seth, with lines around his deep blue eyes that suggested he'd seen difficulties and come through them.

She held out her hand to the dog. "Who is this beautiful creature? I thought fire dogs were Dalmatians."

"This is Max." Gabe fondled the dog's ears, and the animal pressed against his leg. "Max is my seizure-alert dog."

"I'm sorry. I didn't realize—" She stopped, confused. Obviously the private investigator's report hadn't included everything.

"I was injured on duty, and the seizures were an unpleasant aftereffect. So now I spend most of my time training service animals and a couple of days a week training firefighters." He gestured toward the trainees who were waiting for his return. "Join us."

She followed, very aware of Seth walking by her side. Did he think she'd been clumsy? If she had, it hadn't been intentional. Gabe's calm acceptance of his injury must have been hard-won.

And that was another aspect of Seth's firefighting career that she'd think he'd spend more time considering. Did a single parent really have the right to be in such a dangerous profession?

They reached the group of trainees, who looked at her with mild curiosity.

"This is Ms. White," Gabe announced. "She's going to be taking a few photos today. Don't worry about how you look, just how you perform."

A few shot her interested looks, but for the most part the recruits focused their attention on Gabe and Seth. Good, that was how she liked it. She pulled out the camera.

That expression in the trainees' faces when they looked at the brothers intrigued her. Awe came closest to describing it. Gabe and Seth, in their neat blue uniforms, were the men they wanted to be.

"Look sharp, people." Gabe pointed to a long ladder that lay on the ground. "The fifty-foot ladder. How many firefighters to raise it?"

"Six." Several of them answered at once. They were leaning forward, obviously eager to knock themselves out trying to put it up.

She slipped to the side, lifting the camera. She might not understand their ambition, but she didn't need to in order to get a good shot.

The next few moments were a jumble of shouts, groans and straining muscles. The huge ladder seemed to take on a life of its own. It began to sway, almost out of control, and Julie stepped back. She didn't need the warning glance Seth shot her to know it was dangerous.

Then Seth and Gabe took hold of the thing and in an instant it smacked against the building. Seth stepped back, grinning, and dusted off his hands.

"Attitude, people. Attitude. You don't let the Fifty know you're not confident."

It took a second for Julie to realize the Fifty was the ladder. He made it sound like an ally.

Gabe lifted an eyebrow at his brother. "Pretty cocky, aren't you? Let's see how you do against me in a hose relay. Pick your three."

Seth pointed to two of the trainees. Then he pointed at her.

"Oh, no." She didn't know what a hose relay was, and she had no desire to learn.

"Yes." Seth took the camera from her and set it atop the camera bag. "You've been watching long enough. Time to get your hands dirty."

He didn't think she'd do it. He was looking at her with a challenge in his eyes, and he thought she'd turn him down.

She should. She hadn't been physically challenged in years. Mentally and artistically, maybe, but not physically. She was offended at the idea that he'd judge her on the basis of brute strength, but worried at the same time about that strength.

Her eyes narrowed. "Tell me what to do."

He clapped her shoulder the way Gabe had clapped his. It nearly made her stagger.

"All right. Come with me."

Gabe had already picked his team, and they stood waiting.

The relay actually seemed simple enough. Grab the hose, race forward with it on the signal to the next member of the team, and pass it on. The first team across the line Gabe had drawn in the dirt won.

A few minutes later Julie was outfitted in one of the blue jumpsuits. She waited with dancing nervousness on the mark Seth pointed out to her.

Seth had put the two trainees first. She had the third leg and he had the fourth. Obviously he expected her to lose ground that he intended to make up.

She jogged a few steps, loosening up. Seth just

might be in for a surprise. She might not haul fifty-foot ladders, but she did run every day.

Gabe checked the positions of both teams. Then he blew his whistle. The first two trainees raced forward. She watched intently, jogging in place. Obviously the challenge lay in hauling the hose, not in running. The runners sweated and panted as they passed off, almost in a dead heat.

The woman who was second on their team ran toward her, making it look easy until her foot somehow tangled with the hose and she stumbled. There were a few cat-calls, then cheers as she righted herself and charged on.

Like a race at school, Julie told herself. Nothing to be nervous about. The woman reached her, thrusting the hose into her hands.

Don't trip, don't trip. She ran forward, hauling the hose. It felt like a living creature that dragged at her arms, unwilling to move.

Then she realized that the others were cheering for her. Had anyone ever cheered for her before? For some reason the sound pushed her forward. Panting, forcing her legs to move, she reached the line and handed off to Seth.

She leaned over, gasping for breath. The other woman on her team pounded her on the back. "Good job. You gained us a couple of feet." She ran on, cheering Seth as he headed for the finish line.

I did? She pushed herself toward the line as Seth crossed it several feet ahead of his brother.

She was swept into a melee of high fives and

cheers. Seth lifted her off her feet in a hug. "Good job, Julie. Good job. Who would think a little thing like you could run that fast with a hose?"

"Hey, bro, you only won because you brought a ringer with you." Gabe pounded her back. "Good work. Next time you can be on my team."

"No chance." Seth slung his arm around her shoulders in a casual hug. "I saw her first."

She felt a contrary wave of pride. They'd won a race. What difference did that make?

For some reason, Paul's words popped into her mind. "Seeing that I am surrounded by so great a cloud of witnesses, I run the race that is set before me."

There was more realism in that comparison than she'd seen before. You did run faster when you were aware of people cheering you on.

And maybe Seth had taught her something she needed to know about firefighters. That purely visceral response to a physical challenge was part of their everyday life. Without it, they probably couldn't do what they had to do, like raise a fifty-foot ladder, haul a bundle of hose up a flight of stairs or race into a burning building without looking back.

Seth needed that kind of competitive response on the job. But what about turning it off when he went home to his little boy?

Seth caught the pitch Ryan sent his way and tossed the ball underhand to Mary Kate's oldest. The little girl missed the catch but ran shouting after the ball, chased by her younger brother. The ball disappeared into the thick cluster of fallen leaves under the maple tree in Gabe and Nolie's side yard, and they scrambled into the leaves like a pair of puppies.

This might be the last Sunday afternoon picnic of the fall at Nolie's Ark, the farm where Gabe and Nolie raised and trained their service animals. The picnics had become a tradition in the few short months since their wedding. Seth hated seeing it come to an end, but the days were getting cooler already.

The expanse of green lawn was studded here and there with beds filled with the bronze and gold of mums. A couple of miniature horses, a goat and a donkey grazed in the fenced pasture, lifting their heads now and then to watch the Flanagan clan at play.

Seth saw Gabe and Nolie come out of the red barn, and Gabe caught his wife close for a quick kiss before they parted, with Nolie heading toward the kitchen and Gabe coming toward him. Watching them was bitter-sweet.

Would he and Lisa have had that incandescent happiness if she'd lived? Or would the unhappiness that had often shadowed his wife's eyes have gotten worse with the years? He would never know.

"I see she's still taking pictures." Gabe, reaching him, nodded toward the group under the trees. The kids played like puppies, and Julie knelt, her gold sweatshirt blending with the leaves, snapping away.

"That's why she's here." He glanced at the picnic tables, where his mother and Terry were spreading tablecloths. "She'll have to stop long enough to eat, or Mom will be unhappy."

"She gave up the camera at the training academy, didn't she?" Gabe elbowed him. "She surprised you."

"Well, I asked her to participate. I just didn't think she would."

He also hadn't thought she'd do as well as she had. Hauling hose at a dead run wasn't easy, but she'd managed. That deceptively fragile air of hers had thrown him.

"You were trying to scare her off." Gabe's assessment was blunt, as always. It had never been any good trying to put something over on his big brother. "Why?"

He shrugged, not even sure himself why he wanted to discourage Julie. "I guess I don't like the idea of being put on display in some magazine."

"Me, either."

The quiet words made him ashamed. Gabe had more reason than he did to shun the spotlight, but Gabe had conquered his initial frustration with his disability. He even voluntarily went out on speaking engagements with Max, knowing that his actions helped other people with disabilities.

"She's just doing her job." Gabe nodded toward Julie, who had gone over to the tables and was talking to his mother. "Give her a break, will you?"

"I guess you've got a point." Seth bent to pat Max's head. "Maybe I should start cooperating."

Gabe grinned. "A lot of guys would be happy to work with someone who looks like Julie. Loosen up."

"I'll try."

In fact, he'd start trying right now. He crossed the lawn toward the tables, wondering what had drawn a little crowd.

Then he got close enough to see. Julie's laptop. She was showing them the digital photos she'd taken.

He leaned over his cousin Brendan's shoulder to have a look. One photo after another flashed on the small screen like a slide show. Julie leaned back a little, as if to say that she wasn't responsible for how people reacted to her work.

He leaned closer as the pictures she'd taken at Davy's preschool began to show. They were close-ups, most of them, that cut out the background clutter to catch the little faces. Davy, his face so alight with mischief it seemed he'd walk out of the picture, made a mock grab at his father's uniform patch.

"Wow. Julie, these are great."

"Wonderful," his mother breathed. Her eyes misted with tears at a photo of his dad leaning against an engine. Something about the image almost seemed to say that the man and the machine were one.

"Julie, you're a terrific photographer." Brendan smiled at her. "Of course, I guess you already knew that."

Seth looked at Julie to see how she was taking their praise. Her expression grabbed his heart.

She was so obviously both pleased and embarrassed at their words. The woman was such a blend of cool professional expertise and personal—what? He stopped, at a loss for the right word.

Shyness didn't seem to quite fit. He continued to watch her as Nolie announced that the food was ready and everyone began to hustle, setting plates and bowls on the table.

Julie moved the laptop out of the way, but she didn't seem to know whether she should do anything otherwise. She just hung back, awkward.

He touched her elbow, moving her out of the way of Mary Kate and an enormous platter of fried chicken. "Relax, you don't have to help. You're a guest."

Her smile was grateful, as if he'd really done something for her. "I'd like to do my share, but they're so well organized that it's intimidating."

"Believe me, when it comes to getting food on the table, the Flanagans are experts."

Claire, Brendan's fiancée, laughed. "To say nothing of how expert they are at putting it away. Before I got involved with this crowd, I thought Sunday dinner meant a salad and a piece of broiled chicken."

Brendan pulled her into a hug. "You love every minute. Admit it."

"Why I haven't gained ten pounds since meeting you, I'll never know." Claire gave him a quick kiss and shooed him out of the way. "Go help Nolie carry out the coffee urn. You have to do something to earn your meal."

Seth smiled at their interplay. Love. Everyone seemed to be falling in love recently.

But not him. He'd already had his love, and he didn't expect God to send that his way again, but it wasn't fair for Davy to be without a good mother.

That role definitely didn't apply to someone like Julie. But he glanced at her, only to find that Julie was sitting on the ground, intently studying the maple leaf that Davy held out to her.

His son's tiny palms held the leaf carefully, as if he feared he'd tear it. He was smiling into Julie's face, apparently confident that she'd find it equally intriguing.

As for Julie—

Julie looked as if she'd just been handed the best present of her life.

She'd made a big mistake in all her careful planning, Julie thought, pushing back from the table after the enormous meal was finally finished. She hadn't begun to realize how Lisa's child would affect her.

My nephew, she'd wanted to say when Davy had entrusted her with the maple leaf he'd found. *I have as much right to hold you, to love you, as anyone else.*

She hadn't said it, of course. For an instant, tears blurred her eyes. She blinked them quickly away. She couldn't let herself begin imagining that she'd ever have any right to tell Davy who she was. She'd known that from the start. She just hadn't known how much it would hurt.

"See, Julie, see?"

Davy ran ahead toward the pasture fence, while

she and Seth followed along behind. Seth had suggested his son have a nap after dinner, but Davy had shaken that idea off, insisting that Julie had to see the donkey.

At least, she thought that was what he'd said. Davy's language was sometimes difficult for her to understand, although the rest of the Flanagans didn't seem to have trouble interpreting it. Even Mary Kate's two young children were quick to announce what Davy wanted.

"I wish I had that much energy." She watched as the child darted forward, doubled back to check on a dandelion's puffball and then ran ahead of them again.

"I'm telling myself that I can't keep up with him because I ate too much." Seth patted his flat stomach. "But it might just be because I'm getting too old to keep up with a two-year-old."

"Three next week. That's what he told me when I asked how old he is. Three next week."

Her smile lingered on her lips. It was probably silly to be so affected because a small child had shared his discovery that leaves turned color in the fall, but she couldn't help it. So maybe she'd better just concentrate on enjoying this brief span of time with her nephew, instead of mourning that there wouldn't be more.

Actually, it was amazing how relaxed she felt. It could have been that moment of connection with Davy, or the excellent meal or maybe the beautiful surroundings.

Or maybe she was simply happy to be walking across

a field with Seth, watching his son romp through the grass.

Seth's attitude toward her seemed to have changed, and she wasn't sure why. She just knew that slightly edgy watchfulness of his had eased. He accepted her.

"A birthday's pretty special when you're that age." His voice seemed to warm. "Will you still be around then? We'd like to have you come to the party, if so."

"I'll probably be here another week, at least." She said it carefully, fearful of making a commitment she wouldn't be able to keep. "I'd love to come to Davy's birthday party, if you're sure you want me."

"Well, who wouldn't want a professional photographer at a kid's birthday party?" He caught her hand in his, swinging it lightly. "We might actually end up with some pictures we can see, instead of Ryan's out-of-focus blobs."

"No blobs, I promise." She felt ridiculously light-hearted. The warmth of Seth's hand seemed to extend right up her arm.

An outrageous thought flickered tantalizingly through her mind. What if she told him? What if she came right out and told him she was Lisa's sister? He seemed to be accepting her. Maybe he could accept that. If Lisa had told him about her family—

The thought stopped there. She didn't know what Lisa had told him. She only knew what Lisa had told her.

A spasm of pain gripped her heart. She hadn't heard anything from Lisa after that letter saying she was getting married. She hadn't known about Davy.

She hadn't even known about Lisa's death until she'd realized Lisa hadn't drawn any funds from the trust she administered for her. That had roused her concern enough to make her hire the private investigator to find her.

"See, Julie?" Davy danced in front of the pasture fence, waving his arms. "See?"

"I see." She shaded her eyes. "I see the donkey and the goat, but what are those other things?"

"Don't you recognize a horse when you see one, city girl?" Laughter filled Seth's voice. He leaned against the split-rail fence, propping his elbows on it.

"Okay, they do look like horses, but they're no bigger than Max is."

She leaned against the railing next to him. He moved closer, tilting his head toward her. The sunlight brought out red highlights in his brown hair. He'd folded back the sleeves of the flannel shirt he wore, and the light gilded his skin.

"*Miniature horse* is the correct term, I understand. Nolie has started training them."

If he kept using that soft, laughing tone with her, she was in big trouble. "For what? The circus?"

"Believe it or not, she hopes to use them instead of dogs for people who are blind. She says the breed of horses is intelligent and longer-lived than dogs, and should make good guides."

"Seeing-eye horses. Well, I guess that's no more astonishing than anything else I've seen around here. Nolie's Ark, according to the sign."

"She wanted to change it when she and Gabe got married, but he wouldn't agree. He says Nolie's Ark gave him back his life, and he won't have the place called anything else."

Davy was swinging on the bottom rail of the fence, crooning a song softly to himself as he watched the animals.

"I didn't mean to embarrass your brother by mentioning the dog the other day. I didn't know about his disability."

"You didn't embarrass him. He's adjusted to it now. At first—" Seth's face sobered. "When it looked as if Gabe couldn't fight fire any more, we didn't know what to do to help him. Then Nolie gave him a reason to go on living."

She shivered in spite of the warmth of the September sun. "That could have been you."

She regretted it as soon as the words were out. He'd closed her out before when she'd mentioned the dangers of a job like his for a single father.

"I guess it could have." He stared absently at the goat, which seemed to be trying to eat its way through the fence. "You can't think about results like that on the job or you'd be worthless. To fight fire, you need a certain belief in—well, your own invincibility, I guess."

She thought again of the way he'd stepped in to put the heavy ladder up, casually confident in his body's ability to do what was needed. She had to admit, that air of confidence was very compelling.

"But you have a son." She couldn't hold the words back. "If something happened to you—"

He shrugged, pressing his arm against hers and sending another wave of warmth flooding her. "Every firefighter faces that. In my case, I'm a single father, but I do have family." He nodded toward the picnic tables, smiling. "Lots and lots of family. If something happened to me, they'd take over."

"And your wife?" It took an effort to keep her tone casual. "Would her family help out?"

For an instant he didn't move, didn't answer. Her question hung there, like the bumblebee that was poised over a flower at her feet.

"No." His tone brought her gaze to his face, and what she saw there chilled her. "My wife had a mother who left her, a father who controlled her every move and a sister who deserted her. She didn't want to have anything to do with her family. And neither do I."

His words were totally implacable. All the friendly laughter had been wiped from his face. He meant what he said.

So she couldn't tell him the truth. Ever.

Chapter Four

Julie was still struggling with Seth's words when she arrived at the firehouse on Monday. She'd gone over and over it, and she couldn't come to any other conclusion. If Seth knew who she was, he'd hate her.

My wife had...a sister who deserted her. Was that really how Lisa had seen Julie's actions? Pain clutched at her heart. Was it?

She took a deep, steadying breath and willed the pain away, trying to regain her detachment. Lisa was gone, and she couldn't change anything she'd done or neglected to do. She'd concluded a long time ago that they'd both just done what they thought was necessary to survive emotionally.

For her, that meant keeping the shield of her detachment in place. She'd finally figured out how to do that with her father, so that she could see him every month or two, like a dutiful daughter, and still come away whole.

For Lisa, surviving had meant severing the ties completely, so Julie had respected her sister's decision. At least, she'd told herself that was what she was doing when she hadn't attempted to stay in touch.

Had Lisa interpreted that as desertion? Seth had said so, and Seth should know.

The pain flared, like flames shooting up from dying embers. She quenched them again. This wasn't about her pain, or her past.

This was about assuring herself that Davy was in the best situation for him. She'd take that step by methodical step, as if she was researching an article about any child.

On the surface, the answer seemed obvious. Davy had plenty of people who loved him, like the children in the books she'd read to Lisa when they were little.

She and Lisa hadn't quite believed in those big, happy families, but the Flanagans obviously did exist.

Still, she had questions, starting with Seth's determination to continue in what had to be a dangerous job. The Flanagans seemed to take firefighting for granted. She didn't.

She couldn't just accept Seth's view that the rigorous training he and the other firefighters went through would keep them safe. She had to see that for herself—and that meant going with them on a fire call. So far Seth had done an excellent job of evading that request.

No longer. She pulled the door open. Today she'd get his agreement, one way or another.

When she entered the echoing building, Dave Hanratty glanced her way from the back of a rig. He waved with the polishing cloth in his hand, reminding her of what Seth had said about the compulsive cleaning firefighters did.

"Hi, Julie. Here to take some more pictures?"

"Always." She swung her camera bag. "I'd like to talk to Seth first. Is he around?"

"Right here." Seth's voice floated down from the top of the stairs. "Come up and have some coffee."

"Sounds good." She couldn't help contrasting that welcome with the reaction he'd have if he knew who she was.

He didn't know, and he wouldn't. She arranged a smile on her face and walked quickly up the steps.

Seth waited at the top, his smile relaxed. The guardedness he'd shown her at first seemed completely gone now. That should make getting his agreement easier.

"Not running up the steps today?" he asked.

"Thanks, I already had my run this morning." She'd proved she was tougher than she looked that day at the academy, hadn't she? "I realized a long time ago that I had to have an exercise program I could do when I traveled, and you can run most anywhere."

"It suits you."

Before she could decide if that was a compliment, he'd crossed to the stove and lifted the coffeepot that sat there.

"Sure you want this? Ryan made coffee today, and everyone knows he can't boil water."

"Sure. You're drinking it, aren't you?" She pulled out a chair at the scarred table and sat down.

Seth filled one of the heavy white mugs that sat on the counter. "Firefighters develop cast-iron stomachs after a while. Or ulcers."

He brought the mug to her, added a little more of the jet brew to his own cup and sat down opposite her. "I have a cast-iron one, but I have to admit, I like my mother's cooking a lot better than anything I get here."

"Your mother's a great cook."

"She's had plenty of practice." He grinned. "If you think we're bad now, you should have seen us eat when there were four teenage boys in the house."

She enjoyed his smile entirely too much. It would disappear when she told him what she wanted.

"Your cousin Brendan lived with you, I take it." She couldn't be blamed for holding on to the relaxed atmosphere a moment or two longer, could she?

He nodded. "His father was Dad's brother. When Bren's parents died in an accident, there wasn't any question about where he'd live."

Just as there apparently hadn't been any question about where Seth and Davy would live after Lisa had died. They'd moved back to the family home, and life had apparently gone on seamlessly.

Seth raised an eyebrow. "Something wrong? Besides the coffee, I mean."

She'd been quiet too long. "Just thinking about something I want to ask you."

"Ask away."

"Fine. I will. When are you going to take me on a fire call?"

She saw the caution in his eyes, though the smile didn't leave his face.

"We haven't had any fire calls in a couple of days."

"That's an evasion, not an answer."

The smile did disappear then. "Look, when we go out on a call we never know exactly what we're getting into. We can't concentrate on our jobs if we're worried about a civilian getting into trouble."

"I'm not exactly someone you picked out of the crowd. This is my job, too."

"You're not going to remind me that you went up in a fighter jet, are you?" The twinkle reappeared in his eyes, warming her.

"No. But didn't I prove I could handle myself at the fire academy?"

"An hour of training doesn't prepare you for the real thing."

"You expected me to fall apart there, so you'd have an excuse not to take me. Didn't you?"

"If I admit it, will you stop bugging me?"

"No." She'd take that as weakening. "I'm not planning to fight the fire, just photograph it." And see for myself what you face.

"I'd still have to watch out for you."

Something about the way he said the words showed her the source of his reluctance. "You don't want to be responsible for anyone else."

He looked annoyed. "This isn't about me."

"It is when you're the one who gets to say whether I do my job or not. Perhaps Ryan should have been the one the chief picked to babysit me. He'd let me go."

"Ryan's not ready for that kind of responsibility." He shook his head. "Maybe I'm not, either."

"The chief must think you are. Ryan said he's got his eye on you for a promotion."

"Ryan doesn't know what the chief thinks. And if I were—well, I'm not sure I want a promotion."

That startled her. Didn't everyone want to advance in his career?

"Why not?"

He shrugged. "I like where I am. One of the team. You get bumped up a grade, all of a sudden people start looking at you differently."

"The promotion would pay more, wouldn't it?"

"Money's not all that important."

It was a good thing her father couldn't hear his son-in-law talk that way. Money and power—they were Ronald Alexander's twin idols.

"If you were promoted, the job might be safer." For you. For Davy.

A quick gesture dismissed that. "My job isn't all that dangerous."

She saw the opportunity and took it. "Then why won't you take me along?"

For an instant, she thought he was angry. Then he shook his head slowly. "Who would think that under that beautiful exterior there lives a shark?"

"Not a shark." She could only hope she wasn't blushing. *Beautiful.* "Just a determined photojournalist."

He sighed. "All right. If you go through a drill with us, just to be on the safe side, I'll let you ride along."

"Deal," she said quickly, before he could reconsider.

"Deal." He put his hand over hers, as if to seal the bargain.

A wave of warmth spread across her skin from his touch. Seth was looking at her as if they were partners. Friends. She wanted, suddenly, for that to be true.

And that was a dangerous thing to want.

Seth splashed some water on his face, trying to shock himself awake. He'd taken a nap, something he rarely did when he was on duty.

He stretched, glancing at his watch. Well, at least by this time Julie would be gone.

Now why, exactly, did that matter to him?

It didn't. Julie White wasn't anything but a nuisance in his life. An attractive nuisance, it was true, but a nuisance all the same.

He stretched again, opened the door and walked out into the firehouse kitchen. And found Julie still there.

He hesitated for a moment, then went toward the kitchen table where she sat. "Are you taking up permanent residence around here?"

She glanced from the laptop computer, frowning a little. She wore a pair of gold-rimmed glasses that he hadn't seen before, and combined with the frown they made her look serious and efficient. She blinked, as if she'd forgotten where she was.

She glanced at her watch. "I didn't realize it was so late. I'm sorry if I'm getting in the way."

"Relax. You're not in the way." He headed for the coffeepot, stifling a yawn. "Excuse me. I don't know why I bothered taking a nap. It just makes me groggy."

He took a hefty swallow of the coffee, expecting the worst. But the brew actually tasted like coffee. He lowered the cup.

"Ryan didn't make this."

Her smile flickered. "I did."

"Hey, you go around making coffee we can drink, and we may not let you leave." He sat down next to her.

"Actually, cleaning the pot may have had something to do with improving the taste. Were you up late working last night?"

He shook his head. "Davy had a restless night and ended up in bed with me." He grimaced. "Sleeping with that kid is like sleeping with a windmill. His arms and legs are all over the place."

She took off the glasses, holding them absently, as if her mind were miles away. "Does he often sleep with you?"

He wasn't sure whether there was an implied criticism in her words or not. "Not very often. Just if he wakes and seems upset." He shrugged. "I guess even at Davy's age, you can have a bad dream."

"Yes." Her voice was soft, her gaze far away. There

was a tiny line between her brows, and her lips had tightened slightly.

And if he didn't stop looking at her so closely, he might start getting ideas. That would be bad. Julie White was definitely not his type.

Ruth O'Neill, now there was the kind of woman he was looking for. They'd be going on their first date soon, and if things worked out—

He left it there, unaccountably reluctant to follow it further. Ruth was nice, safe, kind. So what if she didn't make him wonder how soft her skin was?

He put the mug down with a thump and focused on Julie's computer screen instead of her face. The screen displayed a photo of one of the preschool kids wearing a fire helmet, and she seemed to be working on it.

"What are you doing with the picture? It already looks terrific to me."

"Not quite. It's the expression I wanted, but the background's a little too cluttered. That's the great thing about shooting in digital."

She clicked the mouse, and the child's face filled the screen. A few more clicks, and a faint shadow disappeared. She smiled at the image, her lips softening.

"You put a lot of love into that, don't you?"

The smile seemed to freeze on her face, and her eyes evaded his. "I love my work. It's my life." A barrier seemed to go up between them.

"Sounds as if your career doesn't leave much time for anything else."

She shrugged, still not looking at him. "I guess not.

I'm traveling a lot, and when I'm home, I'm usually preparing for the next job."

Is that what put that loneliness in your eyes, Julie?

Well, that was a question he wouldn't ask, because that would indicate an interest in Julie he was determined not to feel.

Not your type, he reminded himself again.

She turned back to the computer, and a photograph of Davy came up. The trusting look in his son's eyes put a lump in his throat.

"You're not going to tell me there's anything wrong with that one, are you?"

The line between her brows reappeared. "It's not bad. But it's not exactly what I wanted. I'd like to print a few out for your mother." She shrugged. "Call me a perfectionist, but I want them to be just right. She's been so nice to me."

He shouldn't ask her. Not your type. He was going to, anyway.

"I'm picking Davy up at preschool and taking him to the park. Why don't you meet us there? You can take all the pictures you want."

"Really?" Her smile took his breath away.

"Really."

This was for Mom, he told himself firmly. It wasn't because he wanted to spend more time with Julie.

If she got to the park before Seth and Davy, she would look way too anxious. To be honest, she felt that way, but she shouldn't show it.

She drove slowly down the residential street that Seth had told her would lead to the park. The street was lined with older homes, but there was nothing run-down about the neighborhood. Many of the houses were built of the mellow brick that seemed character-istic of Suffolk, and big old maples shaded lawns meant for children to play. Chrysanthemums and coneflowers crowded flower borders.

School must be out, because groups of children danced along the sidewalks or chased each other through the yards, as if that space was communal property. Interesting, that in a town the size of Suffolk, children still felt safe walking home from school.

She and Lisa had always been driven, slipping from the car to the school in their neat uniforms, seeing nothing of the world outside their schoolrooms.

In a few years, Davy would undoubtedly be like that boy who was racing his friends along the walk, jacket trailing from his backpack, dodging between the pairs of girls who walked more slowly, heads together, talk-ing.

Davy. Her heart skipped a beat. Spending time with him…and Seth at the park…was a plum that had fallen into her lap.

She'd take advantage of this situation, but she had to do it without giving away anything of herself. Seth was altogether too easy to talk to. She had to be care-ful.

There was the park, a larger expanse of green dot-ted with the bright colors and shapes of a child's play area. And there was Seth, pushing Davy on a red plastic swing. Trying to ignore her quickened pulse, she pulled to the curb and got out of the car.

Seth spotted her immediately and waved. He bent over, saying something to Davy, and the child turned, waving his small hand in imitation of his father.

It was useless. She couldn't possibly stop having a reaction to the sight of her nephew. All she could do was try to act her part.

The photographer, that's all she was. Here to take some pictures of Davy as a gift for his grandmother. She started across the grass toward them.

Lord, what am I to do with these feelings for Lisa's child? Am I really meant to walk back out of his life without ever being anything more to him?

She took a deep breath and forced a smile as she neared them. "Hi. Looks like you guys are having fun."

"Swing," Davy said, grinning. "I swing."

"You sure do, Davy-boy." Seth pushed him higher, making Davy squeal and making her heart clench.

That had to be safe, even though it looked scary. They wouldn't have play equipment that wasn't safe in a public park.

Davy swung toward her, his small face lit with laughter. Something about his expression reminded her of Lisa. And that pointed chin—he'd inherited that from his mother, surely.

She realized Seth was watching her. Realized, too, that she'd been staring at his son.

She set her camera bag down and pulled out her camera. Taking pictures, remember? That's why she was here.

"I'm afraid I won't get anything in focus while he's sailing through the air like that."

Maybe Seth would take the hint and have him do something that looked safer.

"Sure." Seth grabbed the swing. "How about showing Julie how you can climb, okay?"

"Okay." Davy held up his arms, and Seth lifted him from the swing to the ground. The moment his tiny sneakers touched the grass, he was off and running toward a pyramid made of plastic stairs and boxes.

"Goodness." She grabbed for the camera bag. "I didn't realize how fast he'd move."

Seth took the camera bag, his hand brushing hers. "Perpetual motion, that's my son." They walked toward the climbing apparatus. "Do you want me to get him to pose?"

"No, let him play. A natural shot is always better. Just harder to get."

She stole a glance at Seth. He'd traded his uniform for a pair of khaki pants and a rust-colored polo shirt that brought out the reddish highlights in his brown hair. Walking next to him made her aware of his height and his solid, masculine strength.

She'd have expected a man like Seth to attract a host of women eager to take on the role of Davy's stepmother. Her heart lurched. Maybe he had and she just didn't know it.

Davy stopped climbing when he reached the level of her head and grinned at her. She snapped off a series of pictures as quickly as the camera would focus.

Seth leaned casually against the apparatus, watching her. "You move pretty fast yourself."

"That's the only way with small children." She studied Davy's small face through the viewfinder. "Take lots of pictures and hope you get some keepers."

"I find it hard to throw any away, even when they're terrible."

"We used to say the film was the cheapest part of the process—now I'm using space on the disk, but the theory's still true. And it's easier to discard what doesn't work than miss a shot that might."

With a quicksilver move, Davy darted down and raced to a shiny plastic climber shaped like a small mountain. Before they reached him, he'd run straight up it. She gasped, heart in her throat.

"Relax." Seth caught her hand in his. "I know it looks slippery, but it's not. He's okay."

Davy balanced at the top. He laughed, flapping his arms as if he'd take off and fly.

"It looks pretty scary to me."

Presumably Seth knew more than she did about what was safe for an almost-three-year-old to do. Still, the urge to protect Davy swept over her, making her want to scoop him up and hold him tight.

Seth stepped up onto the mountain and tugged at her hand. "Come on. You'll see." He scuffed his shoe against the surface. "Safe."

She let him pull her up next to him. Her momentum carried her too far. Her shoes clung to the soft, sticky surface, and she bumped against Seth. His arm went around her in an instant, holding her securely against him.

She suppressed the urge to lean into his strength. She couldn't feel that—couldn't feel anything for Seth. She straightened, groping for something to say that would get them back on an even keel.

"Grown-ups probably aren't allowed on this thing, are they?"

"Probably not." He grinned. "Do you always follow the rules, Ms. White?"

He made it sound boring.

"Most of the time."

All of the time. She'd grown up following the rules, because that was what her father expected, and crossing him was unthinkable.

Davy slid down the side of the mountain on his bottom, running into his father. Seth grabbed him and tossed him into the air, making her breath catch again.

Seth must have heard. He glanced at her. "Too rough for you?" There was a slight edge under his friendly tone, as if he detected a criticism of his parenting.

"He looks so little."

"He's a tough guy, aren't you, Davy?" He tickled the boy, and Davy convulsed in giggles.

"I'll have to take your word for it. I don't know much about children."

She tried to smile. She couldn't afford to offend Seth, not if she wanted to see more of Davy.

"No married friends asking you to babysit?"

She shook her head. He wasn't asking if she was lonely, so why did it feel that way? She had a busy, successful life. Once she was sure her sister's child was all right, she'd return to it with no regrets.

Davy put his arms around his father's neck and leaned his head against Seth's. The unconscious trust of the gesture moved her. Leaving Davy without having regrets was hopeless.

"You don't have any little nieces and nephews running around after you?"

Seth's voice had softened. He couldn't know that he'd just driven a dagger right to her heart.

"Afraid not." Her voice didn't sound natural, even to herself.

"That's too bad." He swung Davy to the ground. "These little monsters add a lot to your life."

She wanted to tell him. The urge was so strong she had to clamp her lips shut on the words until the feeling passed.

That was the trouble with being around Seth. He was the kind of person who was everyone's friend. The kind of person you could trust and confide in.

But she couldn't, and he was looking at her as if he read her feelings on her face.

She swung the camera up, automatically hiding her expression from his observant eyes. Over Seth's shoulder, she caught a glimpse of a man doing the same.

It was a quick impression, gone in an instant. But it sent an unpleasant sensation creeping down her spine.

"What is it?" Seth was looking at her strangely.

"That man over by the soccer field—it looked as if he was taking a picture of us."

Seth glanced in the direction she'd indicated. The man, slinging his camera over his shoulder, strolled away in an unhurried manner.

Seth shrugged. "Lots of people take pictures in the park. You are, and that's perfectly innocent."

Innocent. The word stuck in her heart.

"I guess you're right. I just thought he'd focused on us." She bent over to clear her head, pretending to look for something in the camera bag.

She wasn't perfectly innocent. Maybe she was projecting her own guilty feelings onto other people. She tried to look up at Seth, tried to smile naturally.

He returned her smile, something a little cautious in his eyes. A shiver of panic went through her. How long could she possibly keep this up?

Chapter Five

"Julie." Siobhan Flanagan's face lit with a welcoming smile. "Come in, please. I'm so happy to see you."

"Thank you."

She edged inside the Flanagan house, hoping she wasn't going to run right into Seth. Those moments at the park that afternoon had been emotionally dangerous enough to last her for a while.

"Let me take your jacket." Siobhan touched her arm, drawing her into the warm living room.

"I just wanted to drop off some photos for you." She clutched her camera bag in self-defense. "I can't stay."

A quick look around showed her that the room was empty except for them. Her tension eased slightly.

"Surely you can sit down and have a cup of tea or coffee with me while we look at the pictures. Everyone's out tonight and Davy's in bed." Siobhan smiled. "All this quiet is rare, believe me."

Seth wasn't there. Relief mingled with regret at the news, and she shouldn't have been feeling either of those things.

"If you're sure I'm not intruding, I'd love a cup of tea." A quiet tête-à-tête with Siobhan, the woman who was now Davy's only mother figure, could answer a lot of her questions.

"Of course you're not." Siobhan hung her jacket on the old-fashioned bentwood coat rack that stood just inside the door. "Come along into the kitchen while I make it."

They pushed through a swinging door into the kitchen, where pine cabinets, herbs on the windowsills and a scrubbed pine table created a sense of warmth and acceptance. While Siobhan filled a kettle with water, Julie began spreading photographs on the table-top.

Her fingers lingered on a close-up of Davy wearing that intent expression that reminded her so much of Lisa. She'd printed out an extra one of those. That picture would travel with her from now on.

Adjusting the images and printing out the finished product had been a soothing exercise after those moments at the park. Funny, that something that looked like a very ordinary scene—a man and a woman at a park with a child—could have been filled with so much emotion.

On her part, she reminded herself. No one else had experienced what she'd been feeling. It had been just an ordinary afternoon to Seth and Davy. They wouldn't know that she'd be holding the memory in her heart for good.

"Ah, those are wonderful." Siobhan leaned over the table, her eyes filled with love as she looked at the pictures. "You've caught that child in a way no one else has." Her dark eyes misted. "Thank you, Julie."

She had to choke down a lump in her throat. "You're welcome. He's a very special little boy."

Siobhan turned away to pour the tea and came back to the table with two steaming mugs. She set them carefully away from the prints.

"He is that. Mind, as a grandmother I love them all just as much."

"You're really being a mother to Davy, though, aren't you?" She held her breath, hoping the question didn't offend.

"I've had him since he was six weeks old. Of course, I have lots of help. Seth is more than just a daddy, and the others all pitch in."

"Seth's work schedule must make that difficult, doesn't it?"

Siobhan shrugged, stirring her tea. "Well, we're used to firefighters' schedules. That's all we've ever known in this house."

Three days on and two off, then do it over again, Seth had told her when she'd asked about the working hours. That meant someone had to be taking up the slack at home.

"You're the one who's always here for Davy. He's lucky to have you."

Siobhan nodded. "Of course, if Seth gets married, that will change things."

There was no reason why that casual comment should make her feel as if she'd taken a blow to the stomach. She kept her gaze on the swirling tea and the movement of her spoon.

"I didn't know he was serious about anyone."

"Well, not to say serious. He has this idea that he'll find someone who'll be a companion to him and a good mother to Davy." Her raised eyebrows invited Julie to join her opinion of that.

"You don't think that's a good idea."

"I don't think any of my children should settle for less than a soul mate."

"Maybe he feels he already had that with his wife." She was treading carefully, unsure of the territory. What had Siobhan thought of her sister?

"Maybe." She sounded a little doubtful. "That doesn't mean God doesn't still have a great love in store for him." A soft smile played on Siobhan's lips. "I don't want him to settle for giving less than his whole heart to a woman and receiving the same from her."

The words echoed in her head. A wholehearted love—that was what the Flanagans expected for themselves. They hadn't known the damage that could be done to a person's heart by a loveless childhood.

Had Lisa learned how to love like that when she'd met Seth? Julie hoped so.

The back door swung open. Terry, Seth's younger

sister, came in, slinging an armload of books onto the counter closest to the door. By the looks of the countertop, all the Flanagans did the same.

"Hi, Mom. Hi, Julie. Any more tea in that pot?" Terry leaned over the photos, red curls tumbling around her face. "Wow, these are terrific. Are they for us?"

"They're for me," Siobhan said with mock severity as she poured a cup of tea for her daughter. "I just might share if you're very good."

"Aw, Mom, come on. I bet you'd let Ryan have them. He's the baby. He always gets everything."

Julie was about to offer to make more prints when she realized this was a game they were playing. Siobhan dropped a light kiss on her daughter's hair and set the cup down next to her.

"Stop it now, Teresa. Poor Julie doesn't know what to make of us."

She must be more transparent than she thought if Siobhan saw that so readily. She smiled. "It's nice to see a mother and daughter enjoying each other's company."

Terry looked as if there was a question on the tip of her tongue, but Siobhan headed her off with a comment about the paramedic course that Terry was apparently taking. They talked about the class for a few minutes, giving Julie a chance to regroup.

What was it about these Flanagans? She'd betrayed something about herself with her reactions, and both women had caught it.

She didn't talk about her mother's desertion—didn't even think about it. So why would it come to the surface just because she saw the bond between Siobhan and Terry?

She studied the women's faces. Terry obviously looked more like her father, but there was a certain similarity in the way they talked, the way they gestured, that would betray their relationship to anyone who studied them closely.

Her fingers itched to pull out the camera, as if she could capture that relationship with it. What was she doing here? A sense of loss swept through her. Davy had everything he could need in this house.

"Hey, what's going on in here?" Seth pushed through the swinging door and then stopped when he saw her, his expression changing.

"Hi, Julie." He clearly hadn't expected to see her here, sitting cozily at the table with his mother and sister.

She started to say she was just leaving, but Terry got in first.

"Back from your date already, big brother? It must have really been a dud."

He sent her an annoyed glance. "Ruth had to be at work early tomorrow."

"That's what women say when it hasn't gone well, trust me." Terry elbowed Julie. "Isn't that right, Julie?"

She got up, shaking her head. "I'm not touching that one with a ten-foot pole. I'd better be going. I'm glad you like the photos."

Should she be ashamed of feeling glad that his date apparently hadn't worked out? Well, she was only thinking of what was best for Davy. She hoped.

Siobhan rose, surprising her with a hug. "I can't thank you enough, Julie." She looked at her son. "You're walking Julie to her car, aren't you?"

"I don't need—"

Seth took her hand, momentarily robbing her of speech. "Don't bother to argue. My mother always wins. I'll walk you out."

Seth followed Julie out the front door. She stopped suddenly, looking up at him, at the porch steps.

"You really don't have to walk me out. I'm capable of getting into my own car."

"I know. I know." He held up both hands in a gesture of surrender, wondering if she'd taken offense. "Trouble is, my mother sometimes treats me as if I'm still a little kid."

Her lips twitched. "You let her."

"Hey, she's still the best cook in town." He took her arm. "Please, let me walk you to your car so I don't get into trouble with her."

She nodded, falling into step with him. He saw her rental car now—should have noticed it when he'd pulled in, but she'd parked out on the street instead of coming into the driveway like everyone else did.

"It must be comforting, knowing your mom is there to look after Davy when you're working." Her voice was as soft as the rustle of leaves underfoot.

"It is." His throat tightened, catching him by surprise. He didn't let himself dwell on Lisa's death very often, but the grief was still there. "I don't know what I'd do without her. Without all of them."

"Still, you must sometimes wish—" She let that trail off, but he understood.

"Sometimes you just have to make the best of what life hands you." They'd reached her car and he leaned against it, not ready for the conversation to come to an end.

"Even if it's taken a ninety-degree turn from what you expected." She tilted her head back to look at him, and her face and hair were pale in the moonlight.

"That's for sure." How was it that someone he barely knew could be so understanding? "I thought Lisa and I would be like my sister Mary Kate and her husband by now, with two kids and a mortgage on a house of our own."

"You might still have that with someone else."

He shrugged, wondering why her words made him uncomfortable. After all, it was what he'd been thinking himself.

"You gathered from my nosy sister that I was out on a date tonight." He grimaced. "And that it didn't go well."

"I'm sorry." She shook her head, smiling faintly. "I'm sure you didn't want me to hear that."

"Just promise me you won't use it in the story."

"I promise." She touched his hand. "I'm sorry it didn't work out."

Her light touch was affecting him more than it should. He gave in to the impulse to clasp her hand in his.

"A miscalculation on my part. Ruth is kind, pleasant and agreeable. And it was the most boring dinner I've ever sat through. The worst thing is, she was probably thinking the same thing about me."

Her laugh was low and warm. "I know what you mean. I've been on dates like that. Sometimes I think you both ought to have permission to bail out after the appetizers with no hard feelings."

"That seems a little hasty." He grinned. "Maybe the soup."

"I don't have to stay long if it's a disaster. I don't have family waiting to critique my dates."

He leaned closer, intrigued by the relaxed side she was showing him. Maybe it was worth a disastrous date to get to know Julie this well.

"Yes, but my mother will probably feel sorry enough for me to make my favorite dessert for dinner tomorrow night—apple crumb pie."

"That's a definite advantage."

"Well, I have to confess, my family's not bad, in spite of the kidding that goes on. My brothers and sisters are my best friends."

Some emotion he couldn't read crossed her face at that. "You're lucky."

He nodded. "I am. That's what I want for Davy, too." But Davy wouldn't have that unless he provided him with some brothers and sisters.

"That kind of friendship is really important to you." Julie sounded as if she'd found the key to something that puzzled her.

"I guess it is." He'd never analyzed it, but she was right. All of his friendships were important. Maybe that affected his choices more than he'd realized.

"You're a lucky man." There was a shade of regret in her tone.

"You don't sound very happy about that."

"I am. Just maybe a little envious."

If he leaned toward her any more, they'd be touching. He didn't care.

"You shouldn't be." He inhaled the fresh scent of her hair. "You've got a lot to offer in the friendship department."

And in every other department, too.

"I don't—" Her eyes met his, and whatever she'd been going to say seemed to get lost.

He was lost, too, his common sense forgotten in longing. He spanned the inches between them, and his lips found hers.

She returned the kiss. Nothing touched but their lips, and her kiss was tentative, questioning.

Is this a good idea? Should we be doing this?

He drew away reluctantly. The moonlight reflected in her eyes and tangled in her pale hair, and he wanted to pull her into his arms. He resisted the impulse.

"Good night, Julie." He should be appalled at himself. He wasn't.

"Goodnight." She got into the car quickly, as if to linger would be a mistake. In a moment, she'd driven away.

Julie watched Seth walk down the row of firefighters lined up in front of the engine. His keen gaze inspected each small detail of their protective clothing.

She hadn't seen him in two days. She'd thought that might lessen the impact of that kiss.

It hadn't.

Was he thinking of that, too? If so, he didn't show it. He was all business today. He had been since the moment he'd called to say he'd be directing a drill this morning, if she wanted to participate.

He hadn't said that this was the only way she'd be permitted to go on a fire call with them. He'd already made that clear.

So she'd shown up at the appointed time, dressed as directed in a long-sleeved cotton shirt and cotton pants. Now she wore what felt like a hundred pounds of protective gear over the shirt and pants.

Seth moved a step closer to the end of the line where she stood waiting. Her mouth went dry.

When she'd driven back to the hotel that night, she'd longed to throw everything into her suitcase and disappear from Suffolk entirely. But she hadn't, of course.

She'd made a promise to herself, a promise to God, that she'd be confident of Davy's future before she left. That meant pushing through no matter how miserable she felt, and no matter how many challenges Seth put up for her.

He took another step, then stopped to examine Dave Hanratty's jacket. The jackets all looked the same to her, but apparently he saw something to criticize.

She fidgeted under the weight of the turnout coat. The collar scratched her neck, and she reached up unobtrusively to loosen it.

If putting on all this gear was what it took to go with them on a fire call, she'd do it. Rational or not, she had to see for herself the risks Davy's father chose to run.

Seth stopped in front of her, frowning. "The jacket has to be fastened all the way up."

Ryan, standing next to her, grimaced. "Give Julie a break. She's not really a probie."

"Maybe not, but we don't take shortcuts on safety." Seth's tone was crisp, as if to set a space between them.

He grasped the collar, fastening it securely around her neck. His fingers brushed her skin, and she thought there was an infinitesimal pause before he continued.

"That protects the firefighter's throat. Believe me, nobody wants to be hit in the jugular by flying debris."

She felt Ryan fidget. "Sure you're not taking this lieutenant stuff too seriously, bro?"

Seth sent him a look that was as close to angry as she'd ever seen. "Drop it, Ry." He glanced down the lineup. "You all suited up as if you were going to a picnic. We're going to do it again, and put some hustle into it this time."

A chorus of groans went up at that, but everyone began taking off the gear. She followed suit, wondering.

Judging from Ryan's question, Seth had been put in charge of this drill because he was being considered for promotion. An older man who'd been introduced as the brigade chief leaned against the far wall, watching. He was probably evaluating Seth even as he evaluated the rest of the firefighters.

She still couldn't understand Seth's reluctance to take on a job that would surely make him safer. His explanation had done nothing but raise more questions in her mind.

"Okay, people." Seth raised his voice. "When the bell rings, go for it like it's the real thing."

The next few moments were a blur of movement as people scrambled into their gear. She rushed, nearly toppling onto the concrete floor when she lost her balance shoving her feet into the stiff pants.

Ryan grabbed her arm, steadying her. "Take it easy. You're doing fine."

"Not fine enough."

Her fingers fumbled with the unaccustomed fastenings. She didn't intend to be the last person to reach the lineup. That would just give Seth an excuse for saying she'd slow them down on a call.

She fastened the boots and winced as she snapped the collar into place. She felt Seth's eyes on her, assessing, looking for problems. Pulling on gloves, she scrambled to the line, tired and breathless but not, thank goodness, the last one.

"All right, better." Seth checked his watch. "Much better. What say we do it again and see if we can beat our own time?"

This time the chorus of groans contained a few boos. Seth's eyes flickered. "All right. I'm letting you off the hook this time. Don't get used to it."

Catcalls answered him, and everyone began shrugging out of their gear, a wave of chatter picking up. As she put her borrowed gear back into its battered metal locker, Seth approached.

He planted his hand against the locker next to hers. "What did you think of your first drill?"

"Interesting. You did a good job."

Some emotion darkened Seth's eyes. "It's not really my thing, but the battalion chief insisted I take charge."

She put the boots in place and straightened. It was time to get to the point. "Are you satisfied now that I can go with you on a fire call?"

His reluctance came through before he said a word. It was written in every line of his body.

"A fire scene's a lot different from a drill."

Exasperation made her thump the locker door closed harder than necessary. "You told me if I went through the drill, you'd agree. Are you backing out of your word?"

"No, but—"

"Or is this because of what happened between us the other night?"

She couldn't believe she'd said that. The words seemed to hang in the air between them.

Seth's lips tightened. "What happened between us was inappropriate. I shouldn't have kissed you."

That was what she thought, too, so why did his words hurt? She took a breath, trying for a detachment she didn't feel.

"All right. We both believe it was a mistake. Let's just forget—"

A clatter of equipment made Seth swing away from her. Near the engine, two firefighters glared at each other. She couldn't hear what they were saying, but the tension between them was obvious.

And then Seth was there. He bent to pick up the piece of equipment from the concrete floor, saying something in an easy, joking manner.

She could see the way the others responded to him in the relaxation of their postures. In a moment the flare-up was over, dissolved by his calming presence.

He came back to her, the smile he'd worn for the men slipping away.

She raised an eyebrow at him. "You're comfortable being a buffer, aren't you?"

He shrugged. "Firefighters can grate on each other's nerves sometimes. It's all the time we spend together. I guess I'm pretty good at cooling things off."

"I should think that would make you a good boss."

An irritated frown appeared between his brows. "Being a company lieutenant involves a lot more tough choices than being a friend."

She felt as if he'd handed her a piece to the puzzle

of who he was. It had been there in his reluctance to push his company into another drill, but she hadn't recognized it for what it was.

"You don't like to say no to people, do you? You like being everyone's friend."

"There's nothing wrong with that."

And it's none of your business. He didn't say the words, but they were evident in his tone.

"No, there's not. I envy you. That's a gift." One she'd never had.

"Look, about riding along with us—" He hesitated, obviously still reluctant. "As long as you promise to obey orders, you can go."

She could go. A shiver went down her spine. She'd gotten to know Seth and the others in the short time she'd been here. What would it be like to see them going up against their greatest enemy?

"Thank you."

"Just promise me you'll be careful." He clasped her hand, and something urgent and compelling seemed to flow from his grip. "I don't want anything to happen to you."

She could almost believe his concern was personal, not professional. That probably wasn't a good thing to feel.

Chapter Six

Julie wasn't quite sure what she was doing here. The church hall teemed with people, all intent on enjoying themselves while contributing to a worthy cause. Siobhan had pressed her to come, saying this would show her another side to firefighter culture.

The church festival was being held to raise money for the victims of a house fire. Siobhan had said that firefighters would be out in force to support the cause.

Certainly the Flanagan family was well represented. None of them must have been on duty tonight, since everywhere she looked she seemed to see one. Terry was running a basketball toss in the far corner of the gym, while Siobhan and a young pregnant woman supervised a food stand.

Mary Kate held onto her kids with one hand and sold tickets with the other. She'd spotted Ryan challenging people to participate in some sort of pitching game. As for Seth—

Seth squatted next to Davy, helping him scoop up a plastic toy with a net. Davy's small face was so solemn that it tugged at her heart. She knelt, raising the camera to her face, snapping shots as quickly as possible: Davy's intent look, lips pursed as he decided which duck he wanted. His two-handed effort to scoop up the duck, water spraying onto his face, making him squint. The triumphant grin when he held his prize in his hand. The photos would preserve one small moment of Davy's life for her after she'd gone.

And she'd be gone soon. She'd already taken more photos than she could possibly use. She didn't have an excuse to linger any longer, though her heart said otherwise. She couldn't keep kidding herself, spinning this out to soothe her own wounded heart.

She couldn't offer Davy anything that came near to matching what the Flanagan family gave him. Comfort, security, love—they had it all.

She'd go on the fire call, because she'd promised herself that assurance. After that, she had to leave Suffolk. People probably already wondered why she was still there.

"What are you doing down there?"

Julie looked up, to find Pastor Brendan smiling down at her.

"Just taking a few pictures." She stood up quickly, wondering what his quick eyes had seen.

"You looked as if you were deep in thought." He

gestured at the milling crowd around them. "I was afraid you'd get stepped on."

"It looks as if it's going to be a very successful event. You must be pleased."

He nodded. "With the donations that have already come in, this will be enough to keep the Chambers family going until they can get back on their feet."

She glanced around the gym. "People could have just given the money." That was what she'd have done, presented with a need.

"Instead of going to all this trouble, you mean?" Brendan's eyes twinkled. "Aside from the fact that it's fun, people feel as if they're taking a part in helping. That they're acting out Christ's command to shelter the homeless."

"I guess I hadn't thought of it that way." She hadn't met many people who talked about spiritual matters in such a comfortable way.

"Don't get me wrong, we'll take money, too. But helping others in a tangible way has a spiritual blessing for the giver, as well as the person being helped." He grinned. "Okay, end of sermon."

Maybe she ought to catch a few more of Pastor Brendan's sermons before she left town. "The firefighters are certainly taking part." She'd spotted a number of other people, besides the Flanagan family, in dark-blue uniforms.

"This is important for them." Brendan's smile slipped away. "As the department chaplain, I've seen how they can be affected by the battles they fight. It's good for them to get together in such a positive project."

"They're certainly doing that."

Seth had stepped into a kids' game that had hit a snag, seeming by his very presence to smooth things out. She should be appalled by the way her gaze kept following him, even while she was talking with Brendan.

"Seth enjoys this kind of thing." Brendan clearly knew whom she'd been watching. "He's good with people. He brings out the best in them."

She nodded slowly. "Yes, that's exactly right."

That was what she'd sensed about him—that he brought out the best in everyone he touched. Even her? For a moment she felt disoriented, as if the room had shifted, giving her a new perspective.

Brendan moved off with a murmured excuse. The game had straightened out, and Seth caught Davy's hand and walked toward her. His gaze met hers, he smiled and the room shifted yet again.

Oh, no. She could not have feelings for Seth. There were more reasons than she could count why that was impossible. He'd been her half sister's husband. He didn't know who she was, and if he ever found out, he wouldn't be able to forgive her deception. And if her father found out—

She suppressed her thoughts, trying to produce a normal-looking smile as Seth and Davy approached. He couldn't guess what she'd been thinking.

Besides, Seth was already looking for a nice, ordinary, suburban-mom type of person. That certainly didn't describe her.

"So, are you getting everything you need?" He nodded toward the camera.

He meant the story. Not her personal feelings.

"I'm doing fine." She smiled at Davy, feeling that now-familiar wave of love at the sight of him. "Are you having a good time, Davy?"

He nodded, holding up his prize. "Got a fish."

"I see. It's a very nice one."

"He's easily pleased. When they get older, they get harder to satisfy." He scooped up his son. "Let's sit down and grab a couple of glasses of cider. I'm ready for a rest."

She could make an excuse and move on, but she didn't want to. "Sounds good."

She followed Seth to one of the round tables that had been set up along the side of the gym. A teenager quickly appeared to provide the cider, along with slices of homemade cake. Davy, sitting on his daddy's lap, promptly stuck his fingers into the frosting.

She tried to ignore the fact that her nephew was licking his fingers. "I saw you working with the kids." She nodded toward the game. "You're a good leader."

Seth shrugged. "Maybe. Running a kids' game is different from running a fire company."

"I didn't mean—"

"Yes, you did." He grinned. "That's okay. It's nice that you're interested in my possible promotion. You and my mom ought to join forces."

"She wants you to go for it, does she?"

He nodded, spooning a bit of cake into Davy's mouth. "I understand why she cares." His golden brown eyes focused on her. "I'm not sure why you do."

That might have sounded angry or offended, but it didn't. Seth just seemed interested, as if he were willing to talk with her on a deeper level. As if they were friends.

"I guess it's none of my business." Her gaze rested on Davy's red-gold head, nestled against his father's strong arm. "But I see the relationship you have with your son, and I can't help feeling that you should make sure you're always there for him."

Her throat tightened. Her father had never been there for her or for Lisa, even when he'd been living in the same house. Davy couldn't know how lucky he was.

Seth stroked his son's hair. "There aren't any guarantees, in any event. His mother wasn't doing anything dangerous when we lost her." A muscle twitched in his jaw. "Just driving to the mall."

"I'm sorry." Her voice clutched with grief. She'd never have a chance to make up to Lisa for her failures.

"Thanks." His hand covered hers. "It's good of you to care."

The longing to tell him why she cared swept over her, almost overpowering her judgment.

"Are you giving that child cake again?" Siobhan's voice interrupted whatever she might have said. She reached over Seth's shoulder to wipe frosting from Davy's chin. "He's already had dessert. Twice."

"Mom, it's a special event."

"That's what you always say. You just never want to tell him no."

It was such an echo of what she'd said to him earlier that she looked up, startled.

"I know what you're thinking," he said with mock severity. He looked at his mother. "Julie thinks I'm too fond of being a pal to everyone."

"I never said that," she protested.

Siobhan smiled. "Julie is a wise woman. You ought to listen to her."

Siobhan's gaze rested on their clasped hands, making Julie very aware of his touch. Then she whisked away.

Seth wasn't sure where to look after his mother's comment. Anywhere but at Julie, that was for sure. He shoved the cake away from Davy, ignoring his protests.

"Why don't we go find something more nutritious to eat?" he suggested.

Julie would probably make some excuse to leave the fair, and he couldn't blame her. Mom had been unusually heavy-handed in her matchmaking efforts.

"Good idea. We might find something to counteract the cake and get you out of trouble with your mother."

Julie stood, then bent over Davy with a napkin in

her hand. Her hair flowed like silk over his arm as she wiped the last bit of cake from Davy's face. She tapped the tip of Davy's nose with the napkin, and he grinned at her.

Seth nodded, relieved that she wasn't running for the exit. "We have to spend money, in any event. The family can't rebuild on good wishes."

They walked along the row of stalls offering everything from games to potholders to homemade candy. Church members had outdone themselves this time.

Davy, walking between them, held his hand out to Julie, and she took it, a smile trembling on her lips as she looked at his father.

Davy swung their linked hands, seeming content to watch the crowd. Seth glanced at Julie. This was nice. He didn't know that he'd walked with Davy and a woman this way before. If Lisa had lived, they'd have been doing this. The thought was tinged with sorrow, but not with the weight of grief he'd carried for so long. Maybe he was ready to move on.

But not with Julie. With her casual khakis and that soft aqua sweater, she might look as if she belonged here, but she didn't.

As if she felt his gaze on her, Julie sent him a questioning look. "Did you fight that fire?"

"Yes." She was still looking at him, waiting for more. "A two-story wooden structure, heavily involved by the time the alarm came in. We couldn't save the house, but everyone got out okay, even the family cat." He smiled, remembering. "We found it hiding under what was left of the kids' play set in the yard. That was one lucky cat."

"I guess so. Brendan said they lost everything."

"Pretty much. We pulled out a few pieces of living-room furniture, but that was all we could get." He could hear the regret in his tone.

"You'd have liked to have done more."

He nodded. "Still, they were fortunate. You can always replace property. People are more important than things."

The flash of pain that crossed her face startled him.

"What is it? What's wrong?" He stopped, looking into her green eyes, wanting to fix it, whatever it was. People flowed past them, but that didn't matter.

"Julie?" His fingers brushed her wrist, and he had to fight the urge to hold her hand.

She blinked, then shook her head. "Sorry. I don't know why what you said affected me that way. I was just thinking that my family had the opposite philosophy. My parents put things first, then people."

"I'm sorry." They must have hurt her badly, those parents, to put that look of pain in her eyes.

"Well, that's the past. It's better not to dwell on it." A faint flush tinged her cheeks, and the smile she attempted didn't quite make it to her eyes.

"There's no reason to be embarrassed." He wanted to know more, but this didn't seem the time or the place.

She seemed to pull into herself. "I don't like to reveal myself to the subject of an article. The focus should be on them, not me."

He thought again of the way she seemed to hide behind her camera. "Isn't it okay to show something of yourself to a friend?"

She glanced up at him, startled, her eyes unguarded. His breath seemed to get caught somewhere in his throat. For a moment it was as if they were the only people in the crowded gym.

"I guess. To a friend." Her voice was a breathless whisper that touched his soul.

He was getting interested, way too interested, in Julie. She wasn't the cool customer he'd thought her to be when they'd first met. He couldn't just dismiss her.

But he couldn't let himself start caring about her, either. She wasn't for him.

Julie would be leaving Suffolk as soon as her job was finished. So there couldn't be anything between them.

That was starting to matter more than it should.

If she kept her focus strictly on the computer screen, Julie decided, she wouldn't notice whether Seth came into the firehouse kitchen or not. The article, despite her intent to use it simply as a subterfuge, was turning out to be surprisingly good. Maybe it should see the light of day.

Her fingers paused on the keyboard. Was that wise? If her father saw the piece, was there any way the information could lead him to learn of Davy's existence?

She grappled with that. As far as she knew, her father had never had the slightest interest in what had happened to Lisa after she'd left home. He had wiped her from his life as if she were an unfortunate investment. The chance that he knew who she'd married was slight.

She pressed her lips together. No. Even the slightest chance wasn't worth taking the risk of disturbing Davy's happy life or bringing grief on the Flanagan family. And it was too easy to let something slip, as she'd found out at the church fair.

How on earth had she dropped her guard with Seth, of all people? She shouldn't have said one word about her parents. It wasn't simply a question of raising Seth's suspicions about her, although that was serious enough. She just didn't open her heart that way.

I know I can open my heart to You, Father. I can't seem to get past my fears enough to open it to others.

What would Pastor Brendan say to that spiritual problem? He'd probably have some wise advice, but she'd never know what that would be.

She had to leave Suffolk soon. She'd already known that, and those unguarded moments with Seth had made it abundantly clear. The memories she'd already made of Davy were all she was going to have.

Her throat tightened at the thought, and she had to blink tears from her eyes. She'd never realized how lonely her life was until she'd come to Suffolk and met the Flanagan family. She'd never realized how much she could love a child until she'd come face-to-face with Davy. And now it had to end.

A few more days, that was all. However long it took to go on a fire call with Seth's squad. She'd promised herself that. She glanced at the round clock on the wall above the refrigerator. Would it be today?

Davy's birthday party was this evening. She would have that to remember, at least. The train set she'd bought for him was already wrapped. No one would know how bittersweet it had been to choose that gift, knowing it might be the only one she'd ever buy for him.

Footsteps crossed the rec room, accented by voices. She recognized Seth's easy tone, and her breath quickened in a way that was becoming too familiar.

Terry came in first, followed by Seth and Dave Hanratty. Terry was talking over her shoulder to them, her lively face animated. Terry seemed to do everything with zest.

"All I'm saying is, it wouldn't hurt any of you guys to take a few extra courses. You'd be amazed at how much you don't know."

Dave snorted. "I already know how much I don't know. You're just trying to make me feel worse." He grinned at Julie. "Julie's here. Is it too much to hope you made the coffee today?"

She returned the smile and waved at the pot. "Help yourself. I even brought you a couple of pounds of the good stuff."

Odd, how good their acceptance of her made her feel. It wasn't her. They were friendly to everyone.

"You'll just spoil him," Seth said. "He doesn't know the difference, anyway."

Dave poured coffee into mugs. "I'm learning. If we keep Julie around long enough, I might become a connoisseur."

Terry snorted with laughter. "Yeah, and I might run for president."

She'd miss this interaction when she'd gone back to her normal life. She'd always thought she liked working alone, but she'd never known the kind of camaraderie the firefighters enjoyed.

"You're not leaving any time soon, are you, Julie?" Dave leaned over to look at the photos on her screen. "We're just getting used to having you here."

She sensed Seth's sharpened attention. Because he wanted her to go, or because he wanted her to stay?

The answer to that didn't really matter. She had to go, and Seth could never know why.

"I'll be around a few more days." She kept her voice even with an effort. "I can't give up my big chance to see you guys in action."

"You're seeing the usual routine," Seth said. He propped himself against the refrigerator in his usual easy way. "Somebody called firefighting days of boredom punctuated by moments of sheer terror."

"Any more coffee in that pot?" The brigade chief paused in the doorway, a clipboard in his hand.

She hadn't seen as much of O'Malley as she had the others, but Julie found the man vaguely familiar, all the same. He reminded her of Seth's father, she realized. Same white hair, same air of authority, same comfortable sense of being in control of the situation.

"Sure thing." Seth poured a mug and handed it over.

O'Malley wrapped beefy fingers around the mug. "So, you getting a new car, are you, Seth?"

"A new car?" Seth looked at him blankly. "I haven't finished paying for the one I have."

O'Malley frowned. "That's funny. You sure you haven't applied for a loan?"

"Believe me, that's something I'd know."

Julie glanced from Seth to O'Malley, feeling an odd sense of foreboding. What was going on? She didn't have the right to ask.

O'Malley set his mug onto the scarred tabletop. "That's funny. Somebody called the office earlier. Said he was confirming your job status for a loan."

Seth shook his head. "That's weird. What did you tell him?"

"I just confirmed that you worked here. He started asking some other questions, but I cut him off. Told him to submit them in writing."

Seth looked puzzled; O'Malley looked faintly concerned. Neither of them seemed to feel the worry that crept along Julie's nerves, bringing every sense to attention.

Seth shrugged. "Probably some new gimmick to offer loans or credit cards. You didn't give him my social security number, did you?"

"What do you take me for?"

"That's okay then. If he calls back, tell him to take a hike."

Seth wasn't worried. Of course he wasn't. Someone as open and honest as he was didn't suspect deviousness of others.

She knew better. She was deceiving him, wasn't she? A shiver went down her spine. Her father never hesitated to deceive if it got him something he wanted.

That was ridiculous. Her father couldn't know about Seth or Davy.

Just the thought of Davy ratcheted her tension level upwards. She ought to say something to Seth, something to put him on guard against unexplained phone calls.

But what? She couldn't warn him without giving herself away, and it might all be for nothing. He could be right about that odd call. Besides—

The alarm went off. She froze for a moment, mind processing what it was.

The rest of them were already moving, putting down cups and going to the pole with swift, efficient movements. She stood, her heart pounding. This was it.

Seth grabbed the pole, his gaze meeting hers. His face had tightened. "Still sure you want to do this?"

She nodded, not trusting her voice.

"Let's go, then." He wrapped his legs around the pole and disappeared from sight.

Chapter Seven

Seth had probably hoped this call would lead to something as insignificant as a trash fire. Then he could say that he'd fulfilled his promise to her.

She took a breath, trying not to choke on the dense smoke that shrouded half a city block. If he had hoped that, he'd been disappointed. This time the fire alarm had been the real thing.

She took a cautious step, watching her footing in the tangle of hoses and debris, and aimed the camera at a window belching thick smoke. It wasn't easy to focus when adrenaline pumped through her. Only years of training kept her fingers steady.

The building had probably once been a pristine example of Victorian architecture with its white gingerbread trim and fanciful turrets. Maybe it had been the pride of someone who'd worked his way to the respectability that a house like this represented. Now the gingerbread and the turrets were just so much flammable material, ready to ignite in an instant.

The whole neighborhood had clearly gone downhill over the years. Now a few ramshackle Victorians, split into apartments, shared space with warehouses and garages.

Not enough space. The buildings were so close that a threat to one was a threat to the whole block. All these wooden buildings could go up in a conflagration.

Seth's company had been the first to arrive, but it wasn't the last. Yellow-coated firefighters swarmed over the scene, directing streams of water at the adjoining buildings.

She discovered that it didn't matter how many firefighters there were, or how alike they looked in their uniforms. She could still pick Seth out at a glance. What that said about the state of her emotions, she didn't want to consider.

"Please, Father, protect him."

She whispered the words, knowing no one could hear her in the din. She'd always thought fires crackled. This one roared. How could the firefighters even think with the blaze assaulting every sense?

O'Malley, the brigade chief, stood a few feet away from her, marshalling his forces like a general attacking the enemy. His ruddy face was covered with soot, and debris continued to shower on him periodically. He didn't seem to notice.

Seth and some of the others were preparing to take

a hose line in the door. Seth was in front. He'd be the first one in. Her throat tightened.

Please, Lord, surround them with Your protection. Keep them safe. Please.

"They know what they're doing."

She turned to find Terry standing next to her. Seth's sister wore full turnout gear, and a gray smudge adorned her cheek. The red curl that had slipped out from her helmet looked incongruous.

"You're sure about that?" She could only hope her voice wouldn't belie her light question.

Terry nodded. "Seth's on the nozzle to start. He's smart about fire, and he doesn't take chances." A shadow crossed her eyes. "Unless there's a victim. Then he'd do anything he had to."

Somehow she'd known that about Seth by instinct. He would always put a helpless person's welfare ahead of his own.

"I heard Chief O'Malley say everyone escaped the building." *Thank You, Father.*

Terry nodded. "We've checked them out. Everyone's okay. Upset, of course."

Terry didn't add that the paramedics were remaining on the scene in case a firefighter was injured. That went without saying.

"I'd better get back to my unit." Terry squeezed her arm. "Don't worry. This is a piece of cake."

Obviously Julie wasn't hiding her emotions very well. She nodded, throat tight. Terry started toward her emergency vehicle.

The crew on the steps was waiting for the go-ahead from O'Malley. She focused on Seth, zooming in for a close-up of his face. He looked perfectly calm, supremely confident. He was a man doing what he knew he did well.

Using the telephoto to bring him so close was almost like spying on him. She swung away, catching Chief O'Malley in the camera lens, and gasped. The man was gray beneath the soot streaking his face. Even as she registered that, he started to keel over.

She crossed the few feet between them in an instant, grabbing O'Malley before his face could hit the pavement. He sagged heavily against her.

"Terry!" She shouted against the wail of sirens and the thunder of the fire.

The desperation in her voice must have penetrated. Terry, who'd reached the rear of her emergency unit, swung around and sprinted back.

Terry dropped to her knees next to her. Together they lowered O'Malley to the pavement.

"What happened?" Terry ripped open the chief's jacket to put her stethoscope against his chest.

"I don't know." Julie's teeth seemed to be chattering in spite of the heat that blasted from the fire. "He looked pale, and then just collapsed."

"How is he?" Seth and the rest of his team had reached them almost as quickly as Terry. He leaned over, grasping Julie's shoulder, so that she felt his concern as if it were hers.

"I don't know yet." Terry checked O'Malley's vital

signs with swift competence, her face set beneath the brim of her helmet. "We'll have to take him in to the E.R."

She waved toward her vehicle, and the driver started toward them. Another paramedic was already headed their way, trundling a stretcher over the extended hoses.

Terry's gaze met her brother's. "Looks like you're in charge."

Could everyone see the reluctance in Seth's eyes, or just Julie? The emotion passed in an instant, but she thought she knew what had put it there. He didn't want to send his friends into danger. But he had to.

"Take good care of him." He picked up O'Malley's radio and straightened. "Okay, people. We've got a fire to fight."

She probably ought to move farther away, but she couldn't seem to make her feet carry her. At least Seth wasn't going back into the flames.

Dave Hanratty took the front position on the hose, with Ryan right behind him. They moved up what was left of the porch stairs, a line of humans waging war against a fire-breathing dragon.

Seth raised the radio. "Go."

Seth was doing his job, no matter his reservations. She should do hers. She lifted the camera, trying to capture the moment. Trying not to think about the people she'd come to know and care about in such a short time.

Seth's radio crackled intermittently as she took shot after shot. He was communicating with the men as they moved through the building, coordinating his own crew with one that had gone in the back. His voice was terse but perfectly calm.

Did he realize what a good leader he was? Everyone respected him. Liked him. That respect and liking would carry them along with what he said. Despite how little she knew about firefighting, she understood how important that was when people's lives depended on a split-second decision.

But it had to take a toll on that leader. Seth might sound as if he was only directing a drill, but his hand gripped the radio so tightly that his fingers looked bloodless.

What would happen to him if he made a mistake when other people's lives were in the balance? Her heart cramped at the thought.

Guide his thoughts, Father. Let him feel the reassurance of Your presence.

All that was left was the clean-up. Seth pushed back his helmet for a moment to wipe his forehead and then settled it into place. It didn't pay to relax until they were all safely in the firehouse. People got hurt by letting their guard down too soon.

He did an automatic visual check of each member of his crew. Everyone seemed okay, but he knew only too well their tendency to make light of an injury.

Terry was standing with Julie, watching. That gave

him a good excuse to go over to them. Not that he needed an excuse. He was responsible for Julie, after all.

He hadn't thought about her while the fight went on. Every ounce of concentration had been focused on doing the job.

Still, at some level he'd known she was there. Maybe he didn't want to look too closely at that.

"How's O'Malley?"

Terry smiled. "Not bad. He's grumbling that he's being held against his will. He wants to come back and critique every move you made."

She wouldn't be that relaxed unless O'Malley really was okay. The knot of tension inside him eased.

"He'll find something wrong, you can bet on that. So what happened to him?"

"It looks like a virus. Naturally he didn't admit he wasn't feeling up to par. They're going to keep him overnight to be on the safe side." She nudged Julie. "I told him he owes Julie a steak for keeping his pretty face intact."

That gave him a good reason to inspect Julie with the same care he'd given the men. She looked okay, but her green eyes were shadowed.

"You okay?" He lifted an eyebrow.

"I'm all right." She managed a smile, but it seemed to take an effort.

Terry glanced from him to Julie. "Well, I'm headed back. I'll stop at the hospital and check on O'Malley again before the party."

He watched his sister walk away and then turned back to Julie. She was still looking at him gravely. Differently.

The guys did, too. He'd seen that already. He'd been in charge, at least for a while. That made a difference—whether for good or bad, he couldn't tell yet.

"Are you sure you're okay? The real thing can be pretty overwhelming your first time."

Some of the tension eased in her face. "Do you remember your first fire?"

"Sure thing. I had Dad and Gabe watching my every move, and I felt like I had two left feet. It's a wonder I didn't fall over the hose."

"Obviously you got over that."

He shrugged. "Everyone does, with experience. That, or they don't last."

"I guess if you didn't measure up, it would be best to know that right away."

"I'd hate to see someone walk away without giving himself or herself a fair chance. Just like I'd hate to see anyone get too confident."

Julie glanced toward the smoldering rubble. "I can't imagine getting overconfident about fighting that."

"It happens, and it's dangerous. No two fires are ever the same." He nodded toward the shell of the building. "We didn't save much, but those old wooden floors burn like kindling."

"You did a good job. You put the fire out and no one got hurt."

"I guess that's the definition of a success."

But he hadn't been kidding about O'Malley finding something wrong. Success or not, the battalion chief would analyze Seth's every step, looking for errors. That was the price of being in charge.

There was a smear of dirt on Julie's cheek. He gave in to the temptation to brush it away, but only succeeded in making it worse.

"Sorry." He looked at his grimy hands. "Guess I'm due for a hot shower, and we'd better get a move on." He smiled at her. "Don't forget, we've got a party tonight."

She blinked. "Davy's birthday. How can you possibly manage it? I'd think you'd want to sleep for a week after this."

"Fighting fire is a job. No matter what you do, you have to leave your work behind when you go home to your family."

"Can you do that?" Her eyes held an intensity he didn't understand. "Can you just turn it off for Davy's sake?"

He'd shrug off the question from anyone else, but Julie really seemed to care. She'd moved far enough into their lives that she deserved an honest answer.

"Not always." That was honest, at least. "But I can talk about it with my family. They understand. And Davy will grow up with it, the way all of us did."

"It probably doesn't work that way for everyone."

"No. Sometimes the spouse has problems with the

job. That makes it rough." His thoughts flickered to Lisa, who'd always had problems with it.

"I guess it would," she said slowly. "When that happens, I should think either the job or the marriage would have to go."

He ignored the familiar flicker of pain at the thought. Even if he'd been a plumber, that probably wouldn't have changed things between him and Lisa.

"That happens." He shook his head. "Look, you wanted to know how dangerous the job is. The truth is, it can be dangerous. You can do everything right, follow every rule, and still somebody gets hurt."

Was he arguing with her or with his memory of Lisa? He wasn't sure. He just wanted to make her understand.

"You're saying people learn to live with that." She sounded skeptical.

"I'm saying firefighting is what we live for. I don't think I can analyze it any better than that."

Did she get it? Probably not. Probably only someone who lived with firefighting could really understand.

Well, that didn't matter. A wave of annoyance swept over him. Julie would be gone from his life in a few days, and what she thought shouldn't matter at all. And maybe if he kept telling himself that, he'd believe it.

"You guys going to stand around and talk all day, or you going back to the station?" Dave's grin split his soot-blackened face. He gestured with the pry bar he carried. "Everything's cleaned up, Cap."

"Don't call me that."

Dave let out a hoot of laughter and pounded Seth's back so hard he nearly staggered.

"Not a bad job for your first time in charge. Not bad at all. Come on, let's go."

He tried to hide his grin from Julie. He probably didn't succeed.

She smiled, her green eyes warm with what might have been approval. "Looks like the team thinks you did all right."

"Maybe so."

That was the important thing, he told himself. Not that the warmth of Julie's smile made him feel as if he'd do just about anything to see it again.

Julie still wasn't sure how the Flanagans could make the switch from putting their lives on the line to running a child's birthday party, but here they all were, in various stages of relaxation around the comfortably shabby living room. She stood in the archway, watching as Seth and his father did what appeared to be a play-by-play of the day's fire.

Well, not everyone was relaxing. Davy and his cousins raced through the house, into the kitchen, around through the living room and back again. Sooner or later, she feared, Davy would crash into a doorway trying to keep up with the older ones.

"Relax." Siobhan paused next to her in the archway. "Davy may bump himself, but he's a tough little lad."

"How did you know that's what I was thinking?" She must be transparent to the woman.

Siobhan gave a soft chuckle. "I've seen that worried look before. Worn it myself, often enough, when my hooligans were doing their best to turn their mother's hair gray."

For a moment she felt confused. Siobhan almost sounded as if she had a right to be worried about Davy. Maybe a change of subject was in order.

"I don't know how they do it." She nodded toward the group around the fireplace. Ryan now seemed to be giving his version of the fire, making them laugh. "Go out and put their lives on at risk and then come home and have a normal life."

It wasn't fair to Davy. The thought shot up in her like a flame. What if something happened to Seth? She'd seen for herself how dangerous their work could be.

"Well, they're used to it." Siobhan's clear eyes clouded. "It's worse for those waiting at home, I can tell you. They're so caught up in the adrenaline that they don't think about the danger."

"But you do," Julie said softly. "How do you take it, having all of them involved in something so risky?"

Siobhan clasped her hands together. "Praying helps. You can't live your life dominated by fear, you know."

"'For the Lord has not given us a spirit of fear—'" The verse she relied on so often herself came to her lips.

"That's it exactly."

"Does it ever get easier?" It ought to seem strange, talking so personally with Davy's grandmother, but it felt as natural as breathing.

"No." Siobhan's reply was quick, and then she smiled. "But that's all right. When you love someone, you want him to have the life he's born to have. That's how I get through it."

The words seemed to set up an echo in her heart. The life he was born to have. Davy already had that, didn't he?

"What secrets are you two exchanging?" Seth's voice startled her. He leaned against the archway, looking at them with raised brows.

Siobhan patted his cheek. "If we told you, it wouldn't be a secret, now would it?"

"Now you've really got me worried." He assumed an expression of mock terror. "As if this party wasn't already enough to terrify any sensible man."

"Maybe we'd better get on to the present opening." Siobhan collared one of the small red-haired figures that hurtled past. "That should keep them occupied until supper's ready."

"Pizza, peanut-butter-and-jelly sandwiches, cake and ice cream." Seth smiled at Julie. "Think your stomach can hold up?"

She shuddered. "I assume Davy picked the menu."

"Sure. Mom always let us pick what we wanted for our birthday. The only really bad time was when Terry was a vegetarian for about a minute and a half. She made us all eat tofu." He swung Davy up into his arms. "Come on, big guy. Time for presents."

Davy was clearly too excited to sit in a chair and open his gifts. He ran from one package to another, ripping the paper, and his two cousins tore what he didn't.

No one criticized them, or suggested that this wasn't proper behavior. The adults seemed to enjoy it as much as the kids, oohing and aahing over each gift Davy pulled out.

She didn't remember anything remotely similar from her own childhood. Presents were to be opened sedately, with proper expressions of appreciation. When she was old enough, she'd been required to write her thank-you notes before using or wearing any gift. No one had ever crawled, laughing, through a storm of wrapping paper the way Seth was doing.

She was suddenly lonely. Out of place, as if she pressed her nose against a window pane, looking at what she couldn't have. What she'd never had.

Every person in this room loved Davy. Her throat closed. Including her, but he'd never know that. Everyone loved him. They gave him enough love to make up for anything else that might come his way.

She could never give him anything that would match that. Siobhan had been right. If you loved someone, you let him have the life he was born to lead. This was Davy's life. She had no part in it.

Seth stood, shedding paper, and crossed to her.

"Everything okay? You look a little down. Or is the decibel level getting to you?"

She tried to smile. "It's about the same as the fire siren, isn't it?"

He nodded, his eyes still questioning, as if he saw through that to her heart.

"Hey, Davy, here's another one." Terry shoved a package toward Davy, looking at the card. "It's from Julie."

"You didn't need to bring him something," Seth said.

Yes, I did. But she couldn't say that.

"I wanted to."

Davy ripped the paper, exposing the bright blue engine on the package. "A train, a train!" he shouted, eyes as bright as the engine. "Wow, thank you."

Davy had greeted every gift with "Wow, thank you," even a pair of pajamas. But he did seem genuinely pleased with the train. The clerk at the toy store had assured her it was just the thing for a three-year-old boy.

Seth looked a little stunned. "That's quite a gift. Really, you—"

"I hope it's okay." She said it quickly, not wanting to hear him say that she shouldn't have. Of course she'd spent more than a casual acquaintance should, but she couldn't help herself. "I can exchange it, if he'd rather have something else."

Seth's hand closed over hers. "Not at all. It's perfect. Thank you."

"Open it, Daddy. Set up the train." Davy pulled at the package.

"Davy, I think Grammy has supper almost ready. We can wait until after we eat."

Davy's eyes clouded with tears. "No, no." He stamped his foot. "Want it now."

Julie tensed, waiting for a reprimand. If she'd given him something that would spoil his birthday—

Siobhan got up. "Well, of course you want it now, sweetheart. Daddy and Julie will help you open the train." She glanced at the others. "The rest of you can help get the food on. Maybe by then Davy will be ready to eat, though I doubt it."

"I'm sorry." She said it softly, her words covered by the movement of the rest of the family toward the kitchen. "I didn't mean to mess up the schedule."

Seth's fingers tightened around hers. "Julie, relax. There's no schedule."

"But your mother has supper ready."

"Doesn't matter. It's Davy's birthday. If he wants to open his train, that's what he'll do." He tugged at her hand. "Come on. You gave it to him, so you get to help set it up, like it or not."

They sat on the floor next to Davy, and Seth produced a pocket knife to open the package. Davy leaned against her knee, bombarding her with information about the train that she could barely understand.

She ventured to put her arm around him, feeling the sturdy little body against her. Her heart swelled until she thought it would burst from her body. She loved him so. And she had to walk out of his life.

Maybe, someday, it would be safe to tell them who

she was. Eventually she'd be able to make sure that Davy had his share of her father's estate.

But by then it would be too late to gain his love. To share his childhood. This moment would have to do.

Seth pulled a bundle of tracks from the box. Davy pounced on them and quickly began fitting them together.

"Julie?" Seth's voice was questioning. He leaned toward her across the sea of wrapping paper. "Is everything all right? You look sad."

She tried to smile. She couldn't let him know how deeply she felt this.

"I'm okay. It's just been a much more exciting day than I'm used to."

He reached out, a little tentatively, to touch her cheek. The warmth from that touch went straight to her heart.

Davy was making vrooming noises as he tried to run the engine on the track. Her heart seemed to be making the same sound.

Seth's eyes met hers. She couldn't look away. She couldn't pull her barricades into place. He probably saw how much she'd begun to care, and she couldn't do anything about that.

"Julie." He said her name softly, fingers caressing her cheek. "You—"

"Pizza!" Mary Kate's little boy shouted from the archway, jumping up and down. "Pizza, pizza."

Seth sat back on his heels, and for just a moment he looked as if he'd been hit by something. Then he grinned. "I guess that means the pizza is ready."

Chapter Eight

"You didn't have to help clean up, Julie." Siobhan turned from the sink, drying her hands on a kitchen towel. "Although I have to say I appreciate it, since everyone else seemed to have better things to do."

Julie hung her towel over the edge of the dish rack. "It was a pleasure. I'm sure they'd have helped clean up if they could."

Siobhan chuckled. "You don't have to make excuses for my brood. Those boys are experts when it comes to getting out of kitchen cleanup. And to tell the truth, I'm just as glad Mary Kate took her two home. The excitement level was getting a bit high."

The house had emptied out pretty quickly after the birthday cake and ice cream had been consumed, and Seth had taken a whining Davy upstairs for a bath.

"Davy didn't want it to end."

"No." Siobhan smiled. "But if the splashing I heard is any indication, Seth managed to divert him."

She imagined a smiling Seth, leaning over the bathtub, being thoroughly doused by his little son. She pictured him turning, sending that smile toward her…

No, that part was her overactive imagination. She tried to turn her mind into its usual sensible, practical channels, but it didn't want to go. Instead she seemed to be drifting, oddly suspended between who she thought she was and who she might be.

She wasn't sure what that moment with Seth meant. She hadn't imagined that. In another instant, they'd have been kissing.

She should have made an excuse, like the rest of the family, and gotten out of here the moment the last bite of cake was eaten. Something close to panic swept through her. She was flirting with disaster, letting herself get so close to any of the Flanagans, but especially to Seth.

But she didn't want to go. That was the bottom line. It was so satisfying to be here, to wash dishes with Siobhan, to do the ordinary things she might have done with her mother if she'd had an ordinary life.

To feel wanted. That was what she felt from Siobhan. Wanted. Welcomed. As if she'd come home.

They wouldn't feel that way if they knew who you were, her conscience reminded her.

"Hey, ladies. Look who has come to say goodnight."

She turned. Seth stood just inside the swinging door to the dining room, holding Davy in his arms. Davy, in a pair of stretchy pajamas, his hair wet and cheeks rosy, looked too angelic to be the same little boy who'd been charging through the house after his cousins.

"Which of you had the bath?" Siobhan inquired, crossing the kitchen to kiss Davy's cheek.

"I did, Grammy," Davy crowed, laughing at the joke.

Seth's blue shirt had several damp patches, and his hair was almost as wet as Davy's. His smiling gaze met Julie's, inviting her to join his amusement.

Her breath quickened. She really was in trouble if a simple smile could affect her so much.

"Say night-night to Julie," Seth said. "And thank you for the train."

"Thank you for the train," Davy repeated.

She went to him, wondering if she could kiss him good-night. Davy answered that question by lunging into her arms. She caught him by instinct, inhaling the clean scent of soap and little boy.

He nuzzled against her cheek, making her heart thump. "Want Julie to read my story."

"Davy—" Seth began.

"Julie won't mind doing that." Siobhan smiled at her. "Will you, Julie?"

"No, of course not." Mind taking an opportunity that might never come again? "I'd love to."

"Well, if you're sure." Seth reached for Davy, his

hands tangling with hers. "Come on, little man. I'll give you a horsey ride upstairs."

Siobhan switched off the overhead light. "I'm going to take a book to bed and read until your father gets home. Julie, we loved having you here." She put her arms around her in a quick, warm hug that surprised Julie. "Good night. See you again soon."

Julie fought a battle with her conscience as she mounted the stairs behind Seth and Davy. Siobhan's words had been genuine. But she didn't know who Julie was.

The best thing she could do, for herself and the Flanagans, was to get out of Suffolk as quickly as possible. Unfortunately, her mind and heart were pulling in different directions.

Davy's room was small, with sloping walls and a window seat in an alcove. Every bit of the space had been utilized to turn it into a perfect little boy's room, with shelves for books and toys, a bright blue dresser, even a low rack in the closet just high enough for a three-year-old to reach.

Seth tumbled Davy onto a child-size sleigh bed covered with a quilt in a train motif. Davy giggled, rolling over as Seth pulled the quilt over him. Then he sat up and patted the bed next to him.

"Sit here," he commanded. "Read." He picked up a book from the bedside table and thrust it into Julie's hands. "Train book."

"You can see that you brought the right present." Seth settled at the foot of the bed, leaning on one elbow. "This passion for trains is new. We'll have to go to Strasburg and take a ride on the steam railway."

Davy bounced on the bed. "Ride the train, Daddy. Ride the train."

"Someday soon," Seth said. "Right now Julie's going to read your book, remember?"

"Right." Davy snuggled against her and pulled the book open. "Read."

Seth couldn't know how much it affected her to have Davy snuggled against her so trustingly, hanging on every word of the story. Trust. It was hard to keep her voice steady as she read the adventures of the little blue engine.

The Flanagans all seemed blessed with the ability to trust. At least, she thought it was a blessing. Certainly it was one she'd never experienced. She'd learned through experience she could trust God, but as far as trusting anyone else—

She stumbled over a word, took a breath and collected herself. Seth was wrong to trust her. She was deceiving him. No matter how real this moment felt— reading a bedtime story to Davy, feeling Seth's eyes resting on her warmly—she couldn't forget that it was all a deception.

He and Julie had reached the bottom of the stairs, after being called back by Davy three times for a drink, an addition to his bedtime prayer and another hug and kiss. At any moment, Julie would say she had to leave. He didn't want her to go.

"I should go." Julie's voice was soft, hesitant, and her eyes evaded his. She gestured toward the door, and he caught her hand.

"You don't have to leave yet. Not when the house has finally settled down. You don't know how rare this peaceful time is around here. We have to enjoy it."

She smiled, shaking her head a little, but she let him lead her to the couch in front of the fireplace.

"It's obvious that you and Davy have found the right place, living here."

The fire Dad had started earlier had burned down, the logs falling apart into embers. He put another piece of split wood on, watched the flames flicker around it and sat down next to her.

"True enough." He linked his hands around his knee, his gaze on the fire, but very aware of the woman next to him. "Lisa died when I was still getting used to being a father. I knew I couldn't cope with an infant on my own."

"I'm sorry." Her voice went soft with sympathy. "That must have been very difficult."

He shrugged, uncomfortable as always with getting too close to open emotion. "We got through it." He leaned back, focusing on her. "Then, I guess I couldn't have imagined a day like today, celebrating Davy's third birthday already."

"Thank you for letting me share it." She sounded as if she really meant that. As if being part of a child's birthday party had been a joy to her.

"Hey, it wouldn't have been the same without you.

All those pictures you took—we might actually finally get one of him blowing out the candles."

She smiled. "I think I can guarantee that. I'll go through the shots and print the best ones for you in the next day or two."

"And thanks again for the train. It was the perfect gift. You shouldn't have gone to so much trouble."

She moved a little, as if the praise made her uneasy. "It was nothing. I mean, I wanted to thank all of you for making my job here so easy."

"You can't fool me. There's more to it than that."

She looked startled, almost frightened. "What do you mean?"

He couldn't resist taking her hand between his. "I know you've fallen in love with my son. It's written all over you when you look at him."

"He's too lovable." She seemed to make an effort to keep her tone light. "How could anyone resist him?"

Lovable. That word applied to Julie, too.

For a moment he was shocked at himself. To say that, even to himself, implied that he had feelings for her.

He looked at her, ready to say something light, something that would keep some space between them. And got lost in the depths of her deep green eyes.

"Julie." He murmured her name, forgetting everything but that she was there, close to him, looking at him as if she longed to be in his arms.

He touched her cheek, and her skin was warm and smooth against his fingertips. He tipped her chin up, impelled by an emotion he didn't want to identify, and found her lips with his.

He was swept by a longing and tenderness he couldn't remember ever experiencing. He drew her closer, his arms moving around her, wanting to shelter her against him. Wanting to protect her from that loneliness he sometimes saw in the depths of her eyes.

Her lips moved against his, and he thought they formed his name. He took a breath, trying to regain his senses, then pressed his cheek against hers. Her silky hair caressed his skin, and his nostrils filled with the sweet, fresh scent of her. He didn't want to let her go. He wanted—

Whoa, slow down. He drew back a little, scanning her face. She looked—dazed, he supposed. As if she'd just awakened and not yet shaken off a dream.

"Julie." He said her name again, liking the sound of it on his lips. "You are so beautiful."

He stopped. Luckily she didn't seem to notice.

"No, I'm not." She smiled, putting her palm against his cheek. "But it's very nice of you to say so."

"Beautiful," he said again, dropping a kiss on her hand. "And lovable."

Lovable, there was that word again. He wasn't ready to think about love.

He was attracted to her, deeply attracted. More than that, he admired her—her talent, her courage in tackling whatever was thrown at her. Even that persistence of hers that had initially annoyed him.

But love—

She drew back a little, as if determined to regain some control. "I think you might just be affected by how long it's been since you've dated."

He shook his head. "You're not going to remind me of my disastrous attempt to start dating, are you?"

"I wouldn't do that." The smile she tried for trembled a little on her lips. "But we shouldn't—well, read too much into this. Your wife—"

"I loved Lisa." He said the words slowly. Gravely. Feeling as if he hovered on the brink of telling Julie something he hadn't told anyone else.

She looked at him gravely.

"There's something more, isn't there? Some other reason why you waited so long to look for another relationship."

She was frighteningly intuitive. And he wanted to be honest with her. He owed her honesty, because he could see the vulnerability she tried to hide behind her camera. He could see it in the way she reacted to his family, as if she'd never known a family's love.

He leaned back, wrapping his fingers around hers. If he explained about Lisa, maybe she could understand both his longing and his caution.

"I loved Lisa," he said again. "I realized pretty quickly when we started dating that she'd had a difficult childhood with parents who didn't care about her."

"Abusive parents?" Her voice was strained.

"Not physically, but emotionally. I guess that can hurt a child just as badly."

"Yes," she said softly. "I think it can."

"She was so eager to start a new life. She wanted to leave the old one completely behind, so I didn't press her for details."

He stopped. Had that been wrong, not to push to understand her more?

"She wanted to forget."

He nodded. "I thought I could make her happy, but she never seemed able to be sure she was loved."

"Maybe she couldn't really leave the past behind." Julie's lips trembled on the words, as if she felt that pain.

"I guess not. I thought she should see a doctor about all those emotional ups and downs, but she didn't want to, and I didn't push."

Guilty, a voice said inside his head. You're guilty of not taking care of her.

"How did she feel about being pregnant?"

That he could answer gladly. "She loved it. Every single moment of it, even the morning sickness. I'd never seen her so happy."

He smiled at the memory, but the smile couldn't last. Not when he had to go on to what happened afterward.

He gripped Julie's hand like a lifeline. "Afterward she just seemed to fall into depression. She didn't even want to take care of the baby. My mother had to help. One day she asked Mom to come and stay with the baby. Said she felt better, wanted to go shopping."

Julie put her other hand over his, as if she knew what was coming and wanted to protect him.

"She crashed into a semi on the highway. An accident, they said. But I've always wondered. Maybe it wasn't an accident. Maybe she meant to do it."

Seth's words drove into Julie's heart like a knife. Lisa, beautiful, sensitive Lisa—could she have been so depressed she wanted to end her life?

I can't believe it about her, Lord. But I can't dismiss it, either.

She forced herself to focus. Seth had opened up to her, and she was sure he didn't do that often. She had to respond carefully.

"You can't know that." She gripped his fingers, longing to take his pain away but knowing she couldn't. "It's only natural to blame ourselves when someone we love dies so unexpectedly."

Her throat tightened so much that the last few words sounded choked. She was blaming herself, wasn't she?

Seth clasped her hand in both of his. "You've known that, too."

"Yes." She couldn't tell him that she felt just as guilty for Lisa's death. "I've lost someone I loved, and I blame myself. For what I did. For what I didn't do."

"Then you understand. If I'd forced Lisa to see a doctor about her depression, it might never have happened."

"You don't know that it would have made a difference. If what you fear is true, she might still have done it."

Lisa. Oh, Lisa.

She could read the rejection on his face. "I should have pushed her to see someone."

"You couldn't force her." She clutched his hand. "Listen to yourself, Seth. You couldn't force her to do something she didn't want to do."

"I know that I didn't try hard enough. I didn't force the issue." He shook his head, making a grimace that might have been intended for a smile. "That's me. I always like to keep the peace."

And that probably went a long way toward explaining his reluctance to take on a promotion. He might be forced to make waves if he did.

"I thought it was baby blues, and she'd get better. I thought she'd get better for Davy's sake."

"Anyone would think that." She had to move carefully. "You said that you didn't know much about her family. It's possible there was a family history of bipolar disorder or depression."

He gave her a startled look. "I never thought of that. What makes you think of something like that?"

"I don't know. I'm just trying to point out that there may have been more at work than what you did or didn't do."

She didn't remember much of Lisa's mother, any more than she did of her own. But that might explain the crying jags when she'd stayed in her room for days.

On the other hand, that reaction might simply have been the result of living with her father. She was looking at it through the eyes of the child she'd been.

If she told Seth the truth, would it make things better for him, or worse? If he knew—

She took a breath, trying to analyze what would happen if she told him who she was.

He'd be angry. He might never forgive her. She would bear that, if it meant something positive for Seth and for Davy.

She glanced at Seth. He stared into the fire, but some of the harsh lines had eased out of his face. It was as if, having unburdened himself, he'd found some measure of solace.

If he knew who she was, who Lisa had been, the whole situation would be out of her hands. He could decide to contact her father.

She wouldn't be able to stop him. Even if she warned him, he wouldn't trust her. Why should he, after the way she'd deceived him?

He moved, putting his arm across her shoulders as if he longed for the closeness. "Thank you, Julie. I guess maybe I needed to tell all that to someone."

Just someone. Not you.

"I'm sure it's better to talk about it with someone else than go over and over it in your own mind at four in the morning."

"Yes. That's when it's the worst."

Fortunately he didn't ask how she knew. She'd had plenty of experience in four-in-the-morning soul-searching.

She shouldn't be relying on the strength of Seth's arm behind her. In a way, Lisa had hurt him by not telling him everything about her past. And she was hurting him by not telling him the truth about herself.

But she could do more harm by telling him. It always came back to that. It always came back to what would happen if Ronald Alexander found out he had a grandson.

He'd interfere. She knew that, bone-deep. And he had the money and power to make Seth's life a misery if he didn't cooperate.

And Davy— Fear gripped her at the thought of that lively, happy child being forced to spend time in her father's cold, loveless house.

The thought loomed over her like a boulder about to fall. She didn't have a choice in this. She'd never had.

She had to leave, not telling them who she was, because to do otherwise risked Davy's happiness. She'd just been kidding herself to think she had another option.

"You're very quiet." Seth's arm tightened around her. "Did I scare you away with all this?"

"No, of course not." She tilted her face toward his, knowing she had to reassure him of that, at least. "I'm honored that you picked me to confide in."

"I'm not sure it's much of an honor."

"Yes. It is. It means you consider me a friend. That doesn't happen to me very often." And her heart ached at the thought that they could have been much more to each other, if things had been different.

"Not just a friend," he said softly.

Her heart felt as if it held a shard of ice. "I wish—" She swallowed hard. "I wish I could stay longer. Get to know you better."

Tell you that I love you.

The thought both shocked her and seemed the most natural thing in the world, as if it had been hiding in her heart, sensed but not recognized, for a long time.

He pulled away from her a little. "Do you really have to leave?"

She tried to smile and knew it was an utter failure. "I'm afraid so."

"We'll miss you." He cupped her cheek with his palm for an instant, then let his hand drop. "All of us."

"I wish—"

Her cell phone buzzed, startling her into silence. Who would be calling her here, now? Very few people even had her cell-phone number.

She pulled the phone from her handbag, pressing the button that would let her see who was calling. And her heart stopped.

It was her father's number.

She snapped the phone off quickly, shoving it into the depths of her bag as if her father could look through it and see where she was.

"Don't you want to take that?"

She shook her head. "No. I mean, not now. I'll call back later."

Seth was looking at her as if she were babbling. Maybe she was. She just knew she had to get out of there. She surged to her feet.

"I'm sorry. I have to go." She could only hope panic didn't sound in her voice.

Seth held out his hand. "Will I see you tomorrow?"

"Yes. Tomorrow."

Maybe. Or maybe never again.

Chapter Nine

Seth probably thought she was crazy. Maybe she was.

Julie locked the door to her hotel suite, then went back and jerked the safety chain into place. She dropped her handbag on the desk. The cell phone slid out, looking at her with an accusing eye.

No. Her father never called her. His secretary might, occasionally, to remind her of that monthly dinner with her father, or to cancel if Ronald Alexander was too busy to share a meal with his daughter.

Not that she minded when that happened. It would save her from losing a couple of days to a migraine.

That pattern worked every month to perfection. Several days of not eating before the dinner. Enduring several hours in the company of someone who knew where all her weak points were and used words as skillfully as a surgeon used a scalpel. Then a blinding migraine that left her prostrate. A typical family meal.

She paced across the room to the window. Turned and paced back. The cell phone still lurked on the desk like a snake ready to strike.

Maybe she'd read the number wrong. Picking up the phone gingerly, she checked again. The brief flare of hope was extinguished.

Why was he calling? Worse, did he know where she was? She sank into the desk chair and pressed her fingers against her temples.

Please, Lord. I don't know what to do.

No, that wasn't right. She knew exactly what to do. She had to return the call, because if she didn't, he might get suspicious. She couldn't afford to raise his interest in what his daughter was doing.

She took a deep breath, trying to marshal her thoughts. All her reasoning power seemed to have deserted her.

All right, she had to return the call. That was a given. She had to talk with him without raising any suspicion in his mind or giving anything away about Davy.

Unless he knew already. The boulder that she'd pictured over her head teetered closer to the edge.

He couldn't. But she had to be sure. So she had to call and somehow figure out if he knew, because if he did, she had to warn Seth.

For God has not given us a spirit of fear, but of power, and of love, and of a sound mind.

She wasn't sure about the power. Her father had always wielded that. And at the moment her mind felt anything but sound. But love—that she knew. She loved Davy. She'd do whatever she had to do to keep him safe.

She picked up the phone and dialed the number.

Her father answered on the second ring. That in itself was unusual.

"Julia. I expected you to call me back immediately."

"I'm sorry." Her stomach pitched. She was in the wrong before the conversation had even begun. She took a breath. Control. "I was surprised to receive your call. I hope you're well."

"I'm always well." His voice was cold. "I'm calling to see how you are."

"Fine. I'm fine." Except that her stomach was tied in knots and her head pounded. When had her father ever called just to see how she was?

"I didn't realize you'd left the city. Why didn't you tell me you were going away?"

Because you've never been interested. No, she didn't say things like that. They preserved the facade of a family relationship, and she wouldn't be the one to break it.

"I'm on an assignment for the magazine." Carefully, carefully. Don't offer any extra information.

"One of your little articles." He dismissed her career. "When will you return?"

The question hit a sensitive nerve. Her father

couldn't have known, but he'd managed to zero in on the place she was hurting.

She had no excuses for staying in Suffolk any longer. The fact that it would break her heart to leave didn't count.

"I'll probably be back next week," she said carefully.

"Come and see me on Monday."

"I don't know if I'll—"

"As usual, you disappoint me, Julia." Ice coated his words. "In view of everything I've done for you, surely you can manage to put your family first."

That was what she was trying to do, but he couldn't know that.

"If I'm back in the city then—"

"I'll see you on Monday at three."

The receiver clicked. Ronald Alexander had given an order. That was how he ended every conversation. He'd told her what he required of her. There was nothing else to say.

She clicked the phone off and massaged her temples again. It looked like the migraine would come early this month.

It was time she left, anyway. She knew that. What had happened between her and Seth was too dangerous. Far better to cut it off now, before anyone got hurt.

She rubbed her arms, cold in spite of the warmth of the room. It was too late for that. Hurt was already guaranteed.

Seth's conviction that he was partially to blame for

Lisa's death had echoed in her heart. Her guilt was greater than his could be. She'd known how fragile Lisa was, and she'd failed to protect her.

Those weren't barriers between her and Seth. They were mountains.

"Say that again." Seth leaned forward, elbows on his knees, and stared at Brendan.

Brendan, sitting on the shabby couch in the Flanagan living room the evening after Davy's birthday, glanced from Seth to Mom and Dad. Brendan clearly wasn't happy about the news he'd been forced to break.

"There's a private detective looking into you, Seth." He spread his hands, palms up. "Claire and I weren't able to find out why, but we're sure."

Seth shook his head, trying to clear his fogged brain. It didn't help. He still couldn't make any sense of this.

"Look, Bren, there must be some mistake. Why would anybody want to investigate me?"

Dad frowned. "Tell us exactly what happened, Brendan. Then maybe we can figure this out."

You could always count on Dad to approach problems logically. Since his own logic seemed to be on the fritz, he was thankful for that.

"Right. Well, this guy came to the church office this morning. He claimed to be doing a security clearance check on Seth in connection with a promotion." Brendan's worried expression eased a little. "Obviously he

didn't know about my connection with the department. I knew that didn't wash."

Brendan was right about that. That wasn't how the
department did business, but it could have sounded
plausible to a civilian.

"What did you tell him?" Dad rapped out the question, his sharp tone giving away the depth of his concern.

"As little as possible." Brendan grimaced. "We
danced around each other for a while, with me trying
to get something from him without giving anything
away. Eventually he caught on and beat a quick retreat,
but he'd told me enough to start Claire looking into
him."

He glanced at his fiancée, sitting next to him, and
all the love a man could hold lit his eyes. Claire closed
her fingers over his.

"Makes sense," Dad muttered. They all knew that
smart, efficient Claire, with all her business connec-
tions, was the right person to look into something like
this.

"I did a search, based on the information Brendan got
from the man," Claire said. She handed him a sheet of
copy paper, and Dad got up to look over his shoulder.

"'Harrison Phipps, Private Investigations.' An address in Baltimore." He frowned. "So why is this
Phipps guy interested in me? Or rather, why is—"

The doorbell rang, cutting him off. He glanced
through the front window, saw Julie's rental car at the
curb and beat his mother to the door.

"Hi." Her voice sounded a little breathless.

Well, fair enough. That was how he felt at the sight of her. A wave of pleasure washed over him.

"Hi, yourself."

He reached out to draw her over the threshold. After the way she'd escaped the night before, he'd been afraid he might not see her again.

She held out a manila envelope. "I brought the prints of the birthday photos." She glanced around the circle of concerned faces. "Is something wrong? This looks like a family meeting."

"It is. Brendan and Claire just found out that a private detective is investigating me." He handed her the sheet of paper.

Even saying the words aloud felt odd. That was something that happened in movies, not in real life. Not his life, anyway.

He glanced at Brendan, reading the obvious surprise on his face. Brendan didn't know how far into his life Julie had come. After everything he'd told her the night before, it seemed to most natural thing in the world to share this trouble.

He looked back at Julie and instinctively tightened his grasp on her hand. She was staring at the paper, and she looked as if someone had hit her.

"Hey, relax. It's me on the hot seat, not you."

She seemed to make an effort to focus. "Why? Do you have any idea what brought this on?"

"None. That's what we were just talking about." He nodded toward the family.

Apparently accepting the fact that he'd included Julie in the family circle, they'd begun speculating. Good thing Ryan wasn't here—he'd be coming up with one idea after another, all of them far out of the realm of reality.

"Could it be someone Seth ran into on the job? Someone who thinks the fire department didn't do what it should have?" Claire had pulled out a notebook and was jotting down notes.

"Anything's possible," Dad conceded, "but why zero in on Seth? Their beef would be with the department, not an individual firefighter."

"People don't always think logically in that situation," Brendan said. "They look for someone to blame."

Seth turned his back on them and smiled at Julie, wanting to wipe the concern from her eyes. "See? I have my own private brain trust. They'll figure it out."

She nodded and then shoved the envelope of photos into his hands. "I'd better leave you to it." She spun toward the door.

"You don't have to go—" he began, but she was already hurrying out.

He dropped the envelope on the table and went after her. Maybe he shouldn't have unloaded all this on her, but he'd thought she cared.

"Julie, wait." He caught up with her on the sidewalk. "Don't leave."

She kept moving toward her car, her hair swinging forward to hide her expression from him. "I have to."

"Why?" They'd reached the car, and he caught her

arm as she reached for the door. "What are you so upset about?"

"I'm not."

But he'd seen the expression in her eyes, and it rocked him. Julie was frightened.

"Level with me. What's going on?"

"Nothing." She pulled her arm free. "I'm sorry this is happening to you, but I can't help."

"I didn't ask you to." He'd be angry if he hadn't been so aware of her fear.

She shook her head, lips clamping together. "I'm sorry." She stopped, took a breath. "Really, I am. I wish I knew something that would help."

"It's okay." He captured her hands in his. "I didn't expect you to charge to the rescue. It just seemed natural to let you know what was going on."

She managed a smile, but it obviously took an effort. "I appreciate that. There's—well, there's something I have to do. And I think you'd better get back to your council of war. They'll be wondering where you are."

"Right." He squeezed her hands and then let go. "I'll call you later, okay?"

"Okay." She slid into the car. "We'll talk later."

She said it the way he would soothe Davy when he asked for the impossible. Then she shut the door and pulled away.

For a moment he stood looking after the car, unanswered questions bouncing around in his mind. Something about this strange situation had upset Julie even more than it had him. But what?

He walked slowly back toward the house, to find Brendan waiting for him on the porch. His cousin eyed him cautiously.

"Julie had to leave, did she?"

"Yes." Usually he appreciated what Brendan had to say, but he didn't want to discuss Julie with him.

"Look, Seth—" Brendan looked unhappy with whatever he was thinking.

He shrugged, trying to ease the tension that had settled into his shoulders. "Whatever you want to say, just spill it."

"Okay. How well do you know Julie?"

Whatever he'd expected, it wasn't that. "Pretty well, I'd say. I'd like to know her better. You have a problem with that?"

Brendan put one hand on his shoulder. "I'm not saying there's anything wrong about her. I'm just saying we don't know her very well."

"Seems to me that's my business."

"Fair enough." Brendan took a step back. "But think about it. This craziness with the private detective didn't start until Julie came to town. And a blind man could see how much it upset her."

That came uncomfortably close to what he'd been thinking himself. "It would upset anyone."

But Brendan had a point. Julie had been frightened. Maybe he needed to find out why.

She had to go—now. Julie tossed clothes into her suitcase, not caring whether they were folded or not.

She had to get out of Suffolk now, tonight, before she caused any more damage.

The Flanagans might not have any idea why a private detective would be investigating Seth. But she did. This was a classic Ronald Alexander tactic.

He knew. Or suspected, anyway. It caught her like a punch to the stomach, and she sank down on the bed next to the suitcase. What was she going to do?

She tried to steady herself. Tried not to think about the trust in Seth's eyes being replaced by suspicion.

Think this through logically, she commanded herself. Detachment, that's what she needed. Detachment had always been her strong suit. She'd always been able to sit back, analyze a situation and figure out how best to tell a story with her photographs.

Now she needed to use that same skill. Block the emotion out, because it just clouded the issue.

Was she sure this meant that her father knew about Davy? What about the idea that someone was hoping to sue the fire department for some imagined failure?

The trouble was, she couldn't bring herself to believe this was all a coincidence. The detective agency had been in Baltimore. She hadn't recognized the name, but the location alone was a dead giveaway.

All right, given that her father had hired the man, was knowing about Davy's existence the only possible reason? She drew in a slow breath. Was it possible that her father was investigating her?

That made sense, in a way that only a family as screwed up as hers was could understand. Her father liked to maintain control. If the urge moved him to find out what she did when she was away from Baltimore, the logical step, to him, would be hiring an investigator. Perhaps Seth had only come into it through her relationship with him.

An image flicked into her mind of the man who'd taken their picture that day at the park, and a chill snaked down her spine. How pitifully ironic it would be if her longing to do something for Lisa's child had led her father to him.

She pushed herself to her feet. The only thing to do was go back to Baltimore and confront her father. Find out what he was up to, and then do her best to keep him from hurting anyone else.

A knock at the door stopped her before she could put another armload in the suitcase. She frowned, going to the door and opening it cautiously without removing the chain.

It was Seth. Her heart gave a rebellious lurch.

"Seth. What are you doing here?"

He leaned against the door frame. "Do you think we could talk without a chain between us?"

She ought to leave the chain right where it was, but she couldn't think of any logical reason to do so. She released the chain and opened the door.

"Sorry. Come in."

She took a step back, feeling the need for some space between them. The burden of the secret she carried was so heavy it must show in her face.

He closed the door and stood with his hand still on

the knob. "Look, I just wanted to be sure you're all right. You seemed so upset when you left the house."

Upset. Yes, that pretty much covered it.

"I'm fine." Well, that certainly wasn't enough to make him go away. "It was obviously a family problem. I didn't want to intrude."

"That doesn't really explain why you were so upset."

"I care about you." He ought to hear the ring of truth in that. "All of you," she added hurriedly. "A friend would be upset for another friend. You'd be upset if I were in trouble, wouldn't you?"

His face softened. "I guess that's true."

He was accepting it. She felt as if she could breathe again. "Then you can see why—"

But Seth was looking over her shoulder, his expression tightening. She didn't have to turn to know what he was looking at. Her suitcase, open on the bed.

He took a quick stride toward it, as if to confirm what he was seeing. Then he swung to look at her.

"You're leaving."

Her throat felt tight, and she had to clear it before she could speak. "Something came up."

"And you were going to leave, just like that. Without saying goodbye."

"I—I was going to call you. To say goodbye, I mean."

That didn't sound convincing, even to her. She could see the suspicion in his eyes.

"So it's just a coincidence that you have to leave

just when we've found out about this private detective."

The longing to tell him the truth burned on her tongue. But she couldn't speak. If her father knew about Davy, then Seth would have to know the truth. But if he didn't, if this was all some bizarre effort on her father's part to control her, then it would be far safer for Seth if he didn't.

"I'm sorry you think that." She tried to speak calmly, even though her heart was thudding and her hands felt like ice. "I'm your friend, Seth. I'd never intentionally do anything to hurt you."

"And you didn't have anything to do with hiring this private detective."

"No!" That came out with the conviction of truth. "Of course not."

Something in her tone must have gotten through to him, because his expression eased. "Sorry. It just seemed as if the coincidences were piling up pretty high."

She took a steadying breath, choosing her words as if she were choosing her steps through a minefield.

"I wish I could help." She waved toward the suitcase. "As far as leaving is concerned, I need to see my editor about the story."

She needed to tell her there wouldn't be any story.

"This is goodbye, then." He looked at her steadily, as if assessing the truth of her words.

"I hope not for good. I hope to come back for a few more days after I settle this situation."

She hoped it. She didn't think it would happen, but she did hope it.

She held out her hand to him. "Goodbye for now, Seth. I'm grateful we had this opportunity to work together." The cool tone cost a great deal to achieve.

He studied her face for a long moment. Then he took her hand, clasping it firmly. It felt as if he held her heart.

"Goodbye, Julie. Call and let me know when you're coming back."

"I will." Go, Seth. Please go while I can still hold onto my composure.

He nodded, almost as if he'd heard her thought, and turned toward the door. He took one step before wheeling around and coming toward her.

Before she could guess his intent, he'd grasped her arms and kissed her.

And then he was gone before she could regain her composure enough to say a word.

Chapter Ten

She'd gotten here too quickly, that was all Julie could think. The security gates slid open, and she pulled between the twin pillars that marked the drive to the house. The streets in this section of Baltimore were lined with fine old houses that sat discreetly behind the walls and trees that hid them from view.

The Alexander mansion was generally conceded to be the finest example of Greek Revival architecture in the city. As she pulled to the sweep of gravel at the portico, it struck her for the first time that the mansion looked more like a mausoleum than a home.

Breathe, she reminded herself, and got out of the car. She'd driven through the night to get to the city, too upset after that encounter with Seth to linger in Suffolk. She'd gone straight to her apartment and collapsed into bed, unable to go through any more of her nighttime rituals than a mumbled prayer.

She'd slept like the dead, thank goodness. When the alarm rang she'd called her father's secretary, learned he was spending the day at home and made an appointment to see him at ten.

She glanced at her watch. Nine fifty-five. She raised the heavy brass knocker on the pristine white door and let it fall. Her stomach gave a familiar, protesting lurch.

The door was opened by the current secretary, who murmured in hushed tones appropriate for a mortuary that Mr. Alexander awaited her in the study.

Of course it would be the study. That was where their father called them to express his disapproval for whatever minor infraction had caught his eye. There had always been something. Neither she nor Lisa had ever managed to measure up to his requirements.

She hesitated before the door. *Please, Lord.* She didn't have to finish the prayer. Surely her Heavenly Father knew by now the armor she needed to confront her earthly one.

She straightened, hand on the knob. She wasn't a trembling eight-year-old any longer. She was a successful professional woman with a career of her own. Oddly enough, that didn't make her feel any better.

Then she thought of Davy, and a wave of love swept through her. For him, she could do this. She opened the door.

Her father sat behind the heavily carved mahogany

desk that had looked enormous to her when she was a child. Gray hair, gray suit, gray eyes—everything about Ronald Alexander was gray.

She crossed the Oriental carpet to the visitor's chair. He continued to write as if he hadn't heard her.

She sat down, crossing her ankles with an assumption of poise. "Good morning, Father."

For just an instant she pictured Davy racing toward Seth, screaming, "Daddy, Daddy," at the top of his lungs. That had never happened here.

"Julia." He placed the cap back on the pen before looking at her. "I understood you were not returning until next week." His tone implied that it was inconsiderate to arrive earlier.

"I had to see you right away."

His steel-gray eyebrows lifted. "May I ask why?"

She'd figured out the best way of approaching this—a way that didn't reveal anything about Davy. Now she just had to implement it.

"I want to know why a private investigator is following me around."

He took his time about answering, pinning her with a frosty look. Finally he put his hands flat on the polished surface. "You know the answer to that, don't you? The investigator isn't interested in you. Just in my grandson."

Her throat tightened until it was an effort to breathe. He knew. He knew about Davy. How had he found out?

She struggled to focus. *How* wasn't as important as what he intended to do about it. About Davy.

She had to protect Davy. Fear for him gave strength and passion to her voice. "You can't interfere in his life. I won't let you."

"Really, Julia." He gave her a contemptuous look. "Such dramatics are hardly necessary. I want the same thing you do for the child."

"I don't think that's likely."

He sighed. "I'll spell it out for you. I want to be sure my grandson is in a happy, secure situation. Isn't that what you want? Isn't that the purpose of all your cloak-and-dagger antics?"

"You've known all along what I was doing." When she was a child, she'd thought he could see around corners. Maybe she hadn't been far off.

"I make it my business to keep track of you."

She should have realized that. A man in his position didn't want to be embarrassed by his offspring, particularly not if he had some sensitive business deal pending.

He shrugged, impatient with a moment's silence. "That doesn't matter. What does is that our interests coincide for once. We both want to provide for the boy."

"Without interfering," she said quickly. "He has a good life. There's nothing you or I can give him that he doesn't already have."

"Really, Julia, it's time you outgrew your childish ideas of me. I only want to provide for the boy's future. I won't live forever." A trace of what might have been regret appeared in his eyes. "I want to be sure the child receives his appropriate share of my estate."

"He's a three-year-old. He doesn't need millions."

"In trust for his future, then. That's where you come in."

"How?" All her alarms went up. He wanted something from her.

"Just to continue what you're doing. Spend time with those people. Get to know them. Then report to me on how I can best provide for him. Who should be appointed to administer a trust, for instance."

"His father," she said instantly, and the imprint of Seth's lips seemed to linger on hers.

"Who should handle it if something happened to the father? He's in a dangerous profession, after all." He spread out his hands. "This seems a small enough thing to ask of you."

She looked at him uncertainly. "You give me your word you're not going to interfere."

"I've never found it necessary to lie to you. Do as I ask, and I'll call off the private investigator."

She paused, looking for trouble spots. There didn't seem to be any. Her father was offering to do voluntarily exactly what she might wish.

"If you feel this way about it, I don't see why you don't contact them yourself."

He made a small expression of distaste. "I have no desire to do so. I don't want to know these people your sister preferred to her own family. I certainly don't want them coming to me for money."

"They wouldn't do that."

"Don't be naive. Of course they would. Just do as

I ask. No one need know of the child's connection to me until my will is read." He smiled thinly. "That should make you happy. You've gone to enough trouble to assure that they don't know who you are."

She had. And now she was stuck with that.

Still, this seemed a better outcome than anything she might have come up with. She took a deep breath.

"Very well, Father. I agree."

She'd stayed in the city for several days before making the trip back to Suffolk. She'd thought she could get her head together, regain her composure, go back to the person she'd been before Seth kissed her. Maybe she was as naive as her father insisted.

She parked in front of the Flanagan house and sat for a moment. Dusk shadowed the lawn and made deeper, blacker shadows under the shrubbery. But warm yellow light glowed from the wide windows across the front of the house, inviting her.

Home, she thought. Foolish as it sounded, she felt as if she'd come home.

Well, anything would look welcoming next to that chilly, austere mansion where she'd been so unhappy. She picked up the manila envelope of enlargements she'd brought. That was her excuse for being here.

She slid out of the car, and caution mixed with her anticipation. For all she knew, the Flanagans might have learned who that private detective had been working for. They might have found out who she was.

If that was true, she'd know it the moment she saw

Seth's face. Then she'd have to figure out how to pick up the pieces that remained after the inevitable explosion.

If not, well, she wasn't exactly back where she'd started. She no longer had to worry about her father finding out about Davy. She just had to figure out how to do what he wanted.

Her stomach gave a protesting lurch as she mounted the porch steps. She was taking a risk in believing her father meant what he said. Still, as he'd said, why would he bother to lie to her?

She could still say no to him, even though the thought made her stomach heave. She didn't want to feel like a spy for him. But if she did say no, what might he resort to in order to find out what he wanted?

Trying valiantly to block that out of her thoughts, she rapped at the door.

Seth opened the door, and his face lit with pleasure at the sight of her. "Julie. You're back." He drew her inside, holding onto her hands. "I'm glad you're here."

"Maybe I should have called first." At least Seth's greeting proved that he hadn't learned any unpleasant truths about her while she was gone.

"Don't be silly. You're welcome any time." His hands rested warmly on her shoulders for a moment as he took her jacket.

"It's quiet." She glanced around the living room, empty except for the two of them. A fire burned in the fireplace, and the newspaper tossed to the floor beside a wing chair told her Seth had been relaxing in front of it.

"Unusual, isn't it?" He grinned, ushering her to the couch and sitting down next to her. He studied her face, sobering. "You look tired. Didn't things go the way you expected in Baltimore?"

The question was so on-target that it pierced her heart. If only she could tell him how true that was.

"Not exactly, but it's going to be all right." She hoped and prayed that was true.

She realized she was still holding the envelope. She handed it to him. "Your mother mentioned something about wanting some enlargements of the photos of Davy, so I made some up for her. And a composite. I hope that's okay."

He slid them out. "Okay? She'll be thrilled." He touched the image of his son's face gently. "It's too bad she's not here, but everyone went to a supper at church."

"Everyone but you."

"I'm glad I was home." He put his hand over hers, and his touch traveled straight to her heart.

She'd thought those days apart had cleared her mind. She'd resolved that she couldn't let herself be emotionally involved with Seth when she couldn't be honest with him. That resolution seemed to be hanging by a thread.

"Won't Brendan get after you for skipping?" She tried for a light tone.

He shook his head. "Davy's down with a cold, so I didn't want him up late."

"I'm so sorry." Little kids caught colds, she reminded herself. Don't overreact.

Seth leaned back, turning so that he faced her, just a few inches away. Her breath caught.

"Are we all right? When you left so quickly, I didn't know what to think."

He'd thought she was responsible for the private detective, she remembered. Her heart winced. Did he still harbor suspicions about that?

"I'm sorry it worked out that way. I was upset." She forced a smile. "Partly about work. Partly about you."

"Only partly?"

The smile eased to something more natural. "Well, maybe mostly." She sobered. There had to be a way of getting things on an even keel between them, so that no one got hurt when she left.

Well, no one but her. That was a foregone conclusion.

"I guess I was concerned about how quickly things were moving between us." She said the words carefully. "I like you, but the way our lives are right now—" She gestured, leaving the rest unsaid.

He nodded. "Your job. My job. The fact that I'm a single father."

"Single father of an adorable child. I've grown to care about Davy."

I love him. If only she could be free to say the words.

"I think he's a pretty great kid myself."

"But that makes it even more important to—well,

not rush things." She searched his face. "Do you understand what I mean?"

"I think so." He brushed a strand of hair back from her face, and his knuckles touched her cheek. "You're right. Unfortunately." He smiled. "We'll just have to—"

A sound echoed down the stairwell—a high-pitched, shrill cough that sounded as if Davy were choking. She started to her feet, but before she could take a step, Seth was already at the stairwell. Heart pounding, she raced after him.

Davy. Please, Lord, protect him. The prayer kept time with her running feet.

Seth was already in Davy's room by the time she reached the top. By the dim glow of the night-light, she saw him scoop the child up in his arms. The terrible cough shook Davy's small body.

"What is it? Is he choking?" She felt as if she were choking herself in her fear for him.

Seth brushed past her and charged into the bathroom. "Croup. He's had it before. Come and help me."

Her mind started working again. She hurried into the bathroom. He'd switched on the light already, and he struggled to turn on the faucets while wrapping Davy in his arms.

"Steam," he said abruptly. "We need lots of steam. Turn the faucets to full on and shut the door."

Shaking, she did what he said. Davy was crying, obviously frightened, and the cries just seemed to make that horrible barking sound worse.

Please, Lord, please, Lord. The prayer continued to run through her mind, like a soundtrack playing behind everything else.

Steam began to billow through the small room. Seth leaned closer to the faucet, talking soothingly to Davy.

"It's all right, little guy. We did this before, remember? Just try not to cry. There's my big boy. You'll start to feel better in a minute." He rubbed Davy's back in gentle, soothing circles.

"What else can I do?" she said softly. She felt so helpless. "My car is right outside. Should we take him to the emergency room?"

"Not unless he doesn't respond to the treatment." Seth's eyes met hers, and she saw the fear that darkened them. "He's had this before, poor little guy. We always have to be on guard when he catches a cold."

Davy drooped against Seth's shoulder. He seemed to be responding to the comfort of his father's arms, his father's voice. His crying had eased, and the terrible gasping lessened a little.

Her heart felt as if it had been violently wrung and hung out to dry. How was it possible to feel this way over a child she'd just begun to know?

Seth stroked his head. "He's only half-awake. I need to get some medicine down him before he falls asleep."

"Can I get it for you?" If only she could do something, anything, to help.

"It'll be easier for me to get it than to tell you where to look." He shifted Davy's position. "Let's see if he'll let you hold him while I do that." He tilted his son's face up with a gentle hand. "Hey, buddy. Can Julie hold you for a minute while Daddy gets your medicine? Okay?"

Davy's eyes were half-closed, but he nodded. He held his arms out to Julie.

She took him carefully, afraid that the slightest movement might start him coughing again.

Dear Lord, please protect him. Please make him well. I love him so much that my heart hurts with it.

Davy nuzzled against her, relaxing in her arms as if he'd felt her prayer.

"Here, sit down." Seth eased her down. "Sorry the accommodations aren't any better."

"As long as he's going to be all right." She wrapped her arms around Davy and began making gentle circles on his back the way she'd seen Seth do.

"I'll be back in two minutes." Seth opened the door and slid through, closing it again. The steam billowed and eddied at the rush of air.

Another cough racked Davy's small body. She held him close and prayed. *Please, Lord. Please, Lord.*

"You're going to be fine, Davy." She kept her voice soft. "Just fine."

He stirred against her. "Story," he whispered. "Tell me story."

She remembered Lisa snuggled against her in bed. *Tell me a story, Julie. Make the bad dreams go away.*

Lisa's favorite popped into her mind. It was probably the only children's story she knew by heart.

"Once upon a time, there were three little rabbits," she said softly.

Davy relaxed, his arms going around her neck. She felt his heart beating against her chest, and his breath fluttered against her cheek.

Somehow she managed to go on with the story, in spite of the size of the lump in her throat. She'd promised to make the bad dreams go away for Lisa, but she'd failed.

She wouldn't fail Lisa's child. She would do what was best for Davy, no matter the cost to herself.

She'd gotten Peter Rabbit into the garden when she heard Seth's footsteps on the stairs. She snatched a towel from the rack and used it to shield Davy from the rush of cooler air when he opened the door.

"Better?" Seth knelt next to them, a plastic tube in his hand that contained a red liquid.

"I think so."

"Story," Davy said, his voice a little stronger.

Seth's smile flickered. "Maybe you'd better keep the story going while I get this down him."

She nodded, anticipating a struggle, remembering how she'd hated having medicine forced down her throat when she was a child.

But Davy opened his mouth like a little bird at Seth's coaxing, and the medicine went down with only a tiny cough.

"That's my good boy." He stroked Davy's face.

"Rabbit," Davy murmured. He turned his face into

Julie's blouse and went to sleep between one breath and the next.

"You've got the magic touch," Seth said softly. "He's sound asleep."

"Is he going to be all right?" Her heart still hammered at the memory of that terrible cough.

"Listen to him. He's breathing fine now." He stroked Davy's back again. "We'll keep him in here a few more minutes, and then I can get him back to bed." He looked at her with a question in his face. "You can get out of this steam bath now, if you want."

For the first time it occurred to her that her hair straggled wetly around her face and her clothes were soaked, as were Seth's clothes and Davy's pajamas.

"I'm fine." It didn't matter, as long as Davy was safe. "You're sure he's not going to start up again?"

"I don't think so. I'll get some dry pajamas on him before I take him back to bed."

He stood, turning the faucets off. "Maybe we've got enough steam in here."

"You think?" She managed a smile.

He smiled back, his gaze soft when he looked at her. "I know that was scary. I remember how terrified I was the first time. You were great."

"Only if shaking in my shoes qualifies as great." She stroked Davy's damp curls. "Is this one of those things children outgrow, I hope?"

"Probably." Worry shadowed his eyes. "Some kids who have croup do develop asthma. The pediatrician's keeping an eye on him for that."

A cold hand clutched her heart. Lisa had had asthma. Did he know that? Or was that something she should tell him, if only she could?

"Is there a family history of asthma?" She tried not to sound overly interested.

"Not on my side." He frowned. "Lisa never said anything about any illnesses, and she never had an attack when she was with me."

She should tell him. But she couldn't. Her promise to her father tightened like a noose around her neck.

"Okay, let's see if I can change his pajamas without waking him up."

Seth knelt next to her, and she realized he had a pair of small pajamas in his hand. He must have brought them when he'd come back with the medicine.

He slid Davy's damp top off, his hands brushing against her wet blouse, and she wondered if he could feel her heart pounding. She felt as if he could see the thumping right through her skin, her clothes.

Seth looked up, his face very close to hers. His brown eyes darkened as he met her gaze, and it was as if he knew her thoughts.

She struggled to take a breath. She couldn't kid herself any longer. She couldn't believe that it was possible to do this without emotional involvement.

She'd fallen in love with Seth, and the only future for that love was heartbreak.

Chapter Eleven

"What's the matter, bro? You look like you're letting that paperwork get the better of you." Ryan leaned in the doorway of the tiny battalion chief's office, grinning at Seth.

Seth shoved himself back from the paper-covered desk. "Who knew there were this many forms involved in firefighting?"

"Hey, that's the price of promotion." Ryan seemed to be enjoying his discomfort.

"All I can say is O'Malley better get back here ASAP. Or he'll find nasty letters from headquarters about the way his reports are coming in."

He'd thought O'Malley would be back on duty by the next day, but his virus dragged on, and nobody was predicting how soon he'd be back.

"No word on a replacement?" A little sympathy entered Ryan's voice.

"Headquarters says there's nobody available for another couple of days, at least." He frowned darkly at the desk. "By that time I'll be buried under a mass of papers with a pen clenched between my teeth. You could always give me a hand, you know."

Ryan laughed. "Hey, I feel for you, but not that much." With a casual wave, he walked away.

It figured. Ryan liked the excitement of firefighting, not the dull routine.

Truth time. He'd be making a lot more progress on this stuff if he hadn't spent half the morning thinking about Julie and what had happened the night before.

He ran his hand through his hair and massaged the back of his neck. He couldn't erase the images from his mind. He remembered how she'd looked holding Davy. Her green eyes had been dark with worry and fear.

And love. He couldn't mistake that look. Love for his son. She'd looked at Davy the way Mom did when he was sick. That overwhelming love that made you plead with God to let you be ill instead of him.

He had feelings for Julie. He'd been dancing all around that fact, but he couldn't any longer.

Love? He looked cautiously at the word. After the way he'd failed Lisa, he'd vowed he wouldn't look for love again. He'd figured a nice, mutual affection would be a good basis for a marriage.

Now that seemed stupid. He couldn't skim along on top of the waves when it came to making promises for a lifetime. He'd have to dive into the deep waters for that.

Slow down, take it easy. Stop and look before you leap.

That was good advice. It was how he approached everything in his life. The barriers to a relationship with Julie hadn't gone away. She still lived a life he didn't understand, traveling as her work required. She hadn't given him any indication that she wanted to abandon that.

His duty to his son came first. He couldn't let Davy get too fond of someone who might walk back out of his life. He had to be careful.

Something rebelled inside him. He'd always been the cautious, steady one. Maybe he didn't want to be that any longer.

He heard voices out in the kitchen. One voice in particular—a light, feminine voice. Julie.

Without a second thought, he dropped his pen onto the desk and shoved his chair back. He had to see her.

"You just couldn't stay away." Ryan slung an arm around Julie's shoulder and kissed her cheek. "You're crazy about us, admit it."

He discovered a strong urge to give his baby brother a fat lip.

Julie shoved Ryan away, smiling. "You're right, I couldn't stay away. I had to get a few more pictures of Dave's handsome face."

Dave preened, tossing his head as if he had a mane of hair instead of a crew cut. "I'm ready whenever you are."

Ryan, grinning, gave him a push. "Yeah, that's

likely. Come on, cover boy. There's a polishing rag downstairs with your name on it."

They trooped loudly down the steps. He ought to follow them. He shouldn't stay here alone with Julie.

He crossed the kitchen, pouring himself a cup of coffee he didn't want just so he'd have an excuse to stand next to her. "Did you get some sleep after all the excitement?"

She nodded. "More importantly, did Davy? How is he this morning?"

"He's fine. Just has a case of the sniffles, but Mom's keeping him inside today. When I left, he was trying to build a garage out of blocks for his trains."

She smiled, some of the worry leaving her eyes. "That's good news. Last night was so scary."

"I know." Without planning it, he found he'd put his hand over hers where it rested on the counter. "In case I haven't mentioned it, you did great. You handled Davy like an old pro. Sure you don't have a couple of kids stashed away someplace?"

She shook her head. "Not even one."

"He really responded to you." His fingers caressed her hand. "It would be hard not to."

She looked at him, her eyes as green and mysterious as the sea. "It would be hard not to care." Her voice went soft. "For Davy."

"Just Davy?" He couldn't help the question.

Her pulse fluttered beneath his hand. "I thought we decided it was best to put that on hold for a while."

"Yeah, I guess we did." It was hard to rebel against

his usual caution when Julie held up that warning sign. "Okay, maybe we'll stick to your caring for Davy at the moment."

"That's probably best."

"Right." So why did it feel so wrong?

Julie studied the kitchen table as if it were a fascinating object. "So, did Davy have any more croup episodes during the night?"

"A little coughing now and then, but nothing that even woke him up." He grinned. "Trust me, I know. I slept on the floor in his room."

Her gaze met his again, her expression softening. "You're a good father, Seth Flanagan."

He shrugged, ridiculously pleased by her praise. "No more than most guys. Any father would do that."

"Not any father." A bleak expression swept across her face, and she rubbed her arms as if she were chilled. "Some don't care that much."

What made her look that way? He wanted to know, wanted to push past the barricades and see into her heart instead of staying safely on the outside.

"You're talking about your father, aren't you?"

He smoothed his fingers over her hand. It was hard to be content with that when what he wanted to do was hold her in his arms and kiss away the trouble that shadowed her face.

"I—" She looked startled, pulling back from him as if to bring her shields into place. "I didn't say that."

"You didn't have to. What was your family like, Julie? Why does thinking about them make you sad?"

She pulled away from him entirely, her face smoothing into a polite mask. "I don't know what you mean."

Anger flickered through him. She was shutting him out.

"So you can know all about my family, but I can't know anything about yours, is that it? I thought we were friends. My mistake."

Julie stared, appalled, at the mixture of anger and hurt in Seth's face. She hadn't meant—

"I'm sorry." She reached out to him, only able to think that she wanted to mend this breach. "I didn't intend—"

She stopped. What could she say that wouldn't give away too much of the truth?

He still stared at her, a frown darkening his usually open, friendly face.

"I apologize," she said carefully. "I guess it did sound that way. It's just that my family life wasn't as happy as yours is."

His frown eased away, replaced by a look of concern. "I didn't realize. You never talk about them, but I thought that was just because you were trying to keep things businesslike between us."

"We've gone pretty far from that, haven't we?" Her thoughts flickered to those moments when she'd felt his lips on hers.

He clasped her hand. "Look, I'm sorry. You don't have to tell me anything you don't want to."

"I want to talk about it." To her astonishment, she realized that that was true.

Dangerously so. She wanted to tell Seth everything that was hidden in her heart. But she couldn't do that. If he knew everything, their friendship would be blasted to oblivion.

"Okay." He gave her that lopsided smile that made her heart swell. "Sit." He pulled out a chair. "Have coffee. Talk. That's what we do around here."

She sat down, accepting the mug of coffee he handed her. "You've had a lot of practice listening to people."

He considered that, head tilted a little to one side as he sat down next to her. He put his elbows on the table, and his upper arm pressed against hers, all warmth and muscle.

"I guess. Maybe that comes from where I landed in the family. When you're in the middle, you end up listening to everybody."

"You were the buffer."

"That I was." There was an echo of his father's faint brogue in the way he said the words. "Now, you wouldn't be changing the subject, would you?"

She shook her head. She had to tell him a little of it, enough so that he understood, not enough to let him put the pieces together.

"My mother died when I was about Davy's age. I don't remember much about her."

Did that mean that when she'd gone from Davy's life, he wouldn't remember her? The thought made her heart ache.

"I'm sorry." His hand captured hers. "That's rough. Maybe even harder than Davy's situation. He's always had Mom. You didn't have a grandmother to stand in?"

"None that were available." He wouldn't understand grandparents who didn't want to be in their grandchildren's lives.

"So it was just you and your father."

She nodded. And a battalion of servants, but maybe it was better not to say that.

"I'd think you'd have been close."

"You'd think that, wouldn't you? But my father wasn't really into children." Her voice tightened. "I'm afraid he saw me as something of a nuisance."

"You're anything but that." His fingers were warm on hers.

She cleared her throat. It would be so easy to relax into the warm sympathy that poured from Seth. So easy, and so dangerous.

"Well, anyway, my father remarried when I was still very young. I suppose he thought I should be provided with a mother." She stopped, realizing that was what Siobhan had told her Seth intended to do. She felt color rush to her cheeks. "I didn't mean to sound—"

"Forget it." His voice deepened. "I already know what an idiot I was, thinking that way. I did have good intentions, but you know where that's supposed to lead."

"I'm not sure what my father's intentions were. I

just know that the marriage was a very unhappy one. And I always felt caught in the middle. And unnecessary."

Trying to protect Lisa. But she couldn't tell him that.

"No child should ever feel that way. People don't think about what their quarreling does to a child."

He'd drawn the obvious conclusion. He probably hadn't ever experienced the icy silences and cutting remarks that her father and Lisa's mother had specialized in. A few shouts might have relieved the tension.

She managed a smile. "Well, none of the Flanagans ever felt that way, I'm sure. But your family is tough to live up to, you know that?"

His lips curved. "Please don't tell them that. They already think they have the right to interfere in my life as much as they want."

She'd eased past all the things she couldn't say. Now she just had to wrap this up quickly.

"Well, anyway, that's the short version of my childhood. But I got past it. People do. I just tend not to talk about it much."

"You ended up smart, talented and successful in spite of it. Your father must be proud of you."

That was certainly the last word he'd use to describe how he felt about her.

She shrugged. "I guess. We're not close. I see him once a month for dinner, but it's a pretty stilted affair."

He wouldn't understand a relationship in which a daughter got a migraine every time she was exposed to her father's presence.

"End of story?" He raised his eyebrows, as if he knew there were things she wasn't telling him.

"Pretty much." She took a breath, feeling as if she'd unloaded a small share of her burden. "Thanks for listening."

He wrapped both hands around hers, making her feel warmed and sheltered. "Anytime." The words were soft, intimate.

Her heart lurched. Hadn't she just been telling herself how dangerous it was to get this close to Seth? She glanced at the door. Someone could come bursting in at any moment to break this up, but all was quiet. She sought for something that would get them onto safer territory.

"I forgot to ask you last night. What happened with that private detective you thought was investigating you? Did you find out what that was about?"

He shook his head, apparently accepting the change of subject. "Dad still thinks it's someone with a beef against the department."

Seth sounded as if he'd brushed off the whole business. That was safer for her, certainly, but it showed how innocent he was when it came to dealing with someone like her father.

"So you never tried to talk to the man?"

"Sure I did." His look seemed to ask what she took him for. "Brendan and I tracked him down at the motel where he'd been staying."

It took an effort to speak naturally. "You talked to him, then." *Did he tell you anything that might lead to me?*

"He'd already checked out by the time we got there."

Relief swept over her. "So that was a dead end."

"We had the name and address of his firm. Claire had found that out, so I called him."

Maybe her relief had been premature. "What did he say?"

He shrugged. "He wouldn't give me the time of day. Completely stonewalled me. So, short of going to Baltimore and beating the guy up, I guess we'll never know."

She felt her face freeze at his easy mention of the city. She'd forgotten that if he had the address, he'd know that. And know that she'd also been in Baltimore.

"Hey, don't look like that. I wouldn't really beat him up. I haven't hit anyone since grade school, although Ryan sometimes gives me the urge."

"I wasn't worried about that." Maybe it was better to bring the subject up herself than wait for him to do it. "I guess I didn't realize the man was from Baltimore. That's where I live, when I'm not traveling."

"Yes. I know." She felt his eyes on her face. "I don't suppose you've ever heard of this agency of his."

"I'm afraid I've never had occasion to look into detective agencies. Nobody's ever sued me for taking an unflattering photo. Or for failing to shovel my walk in winter."

He nodded, seeming to accept her words at face value. "Well, I hope nobody's planning to sue me.

Seems like if I'd done something worth getting sued over, I'd know it."

"I'm sure it's nothing. You'll probably never hear about this man again."

If her father kept his word, that should be true. The detective was out of the picture.

And she was supposed to take his place.

Her first effort to play at being a private detective was working out much more smoothly than she'd expected. She'd arrived at the new chrome-and-glass downtown building that housed the fire-department offices with very little expectation of success.

But when she'd told the information officer that she needed to do some fact-checking for her article, he'd readily given her all the access at his command. Apparently, having the chief's approval for the magazine piece meant that all doors were open to her.

So she sat alone in the office he'd shown her to, a bland, beige square whose bulletin board held a poster for a fire-department picnic that had taken place in August, and a command that all department employees were to be up-to-date on the latest public-safety regulations.

The desktop computer was open to the department's personnel files. She felt like a spy.

Still, if she didn't get the information her father wanted, he was perfectly prepared to start another investigation. This time he'd hire someone who wouldn't be so easily caught.

She glanced at the hallway beyond the open door. People walked back and forth across her line of vision, some of them men and women in uniform, others civilians.

Some instinct to hide what she was doing made her want to close the door. Bar it, for that matter, but that would only arouse suspicion where there'd been none. She had to act as if this were a perfectly honest, aboveboard operation, even though she felt like a sneak.

She started copying the relevant files to disk. That way she could get out of here quickly, before someone who knew the Flanagans spotted her and decided to mention it to one of them. She could take the files back to the hotel and go over them at leisure, deciding what to pass on to her father.

She frowned at the screen, a headache beginning to build behind her eyes. Some of the facts her father had asked for surprised her.

Why did he want detailed financial information on all the Flanagans, for instance? What difference did it make to anything that Joe Flanagan had borrowed money from his credit union thirty years ago to add on to his house?

Administering a trust wasn't always an easy job, as she knew from handling the one their aunt had left to Lisa. If he was considering which person would do that best should something happen to Seth—

Her mind cringed away from the thought of a world without Seth in it. Each little piece she learned about him only made her admire him more. Respect him more. Love him more.

She massaged her temples, half wishing she could massage the memories away. How had she dropped her guard enough to tell Seth so much about her life? Oh, she'd tried to censor what she said, but the revealing thing was how much more she'd longed to say.

She didn't do that. She'd learned through bitter experience that the daughter of a wealthy, prominent man was considered fair game. Her father had been casually cruel about her attempts at romance when he'd had to scotch the article a college boyfriend had tried to peddle to the tabloids.

She'd learned to keep up her defenses. Unfortunately, she didn't seem to have any where Seth was concerned. She clicked the command to copy his information, averting her eyes as if that would make her less culpable.

A footstep sounded behind her. The information officer, no doubt, come to see how she was doing.

"I'm almost finished." She swung the chair around.

And saw Seth standing inside the door, looking at her with a mix of suspicion and anger in his eyes.

"What are you doing with my personnel records?"

Chapter Twelve

Julie's heart seemed to slam against her ribs with every beat. It took her a moment just to start breathing again, and in that moment Seth had stepped inside and closed the door behind him, cutting off any possible retreat.

She'd seen that grim expression on his face before, when he'd fought the fire. When fire had been the enemy. Now she was the enemy.

"What are you doing with my personnel file?" he repeated, suspicion hardening his voice.

She tried to gather her scattered wits. "Research." It had worked with the information officer, but she didn't think it would work with Seth. "Why are you here? I thought you were off this afternoon."

He took a step closer, so that he stood within inches, frowning down at her. "Trying to bug them into assigning someone to take O'Malley's place, not that it matters. What kind of research makes you snoop into my personnel file?"

"I'm not—" Somehow she didn't think she could say convincingly that she wasn't snooping. "I'm doing some fact-checking for my article, that's all."

His frown didn't lighten. He wasn't buying it.

"This is the kind of thing that private detective was trying to get. You're working with him, aren't you?"

"No." She wasn't, not really, but she was afraid skirting the truth wouldn't help her now.

Seth planted one hand on the desk and leaned toward her. His golden brown eyes had gone hard, and all the easy friendliness was gone from his face.

"I'm finding it hard to believe that, Julie. You told me you didn't know anything about that detective. That wasn't true, was it?"

Her stomach gave a protesting lurch. It was all going to come out, and Seth would hate her. She clasped the chair arms, her hands rigid with strain.

"I didn't know anything about him, not then. Not until afterward."

"You know now."

She couldn't hide from this. She couldn't run away.

"I know who hired him." Her throat felt too parched for speech, but she forced the words out. "My father." She couldn't look at him. "Lisa's father."

He drew in a harsh breath. "Lisa—my wife, Lisa." He said the words numbly, as if he'd heard but couldn't comprehend.

She nodded, forcing herself to look at him. He looked as stunned as if she'd hit him with something. Maybe she had.

"Lisa was my half sister. We have the same father."

He shook his head slowly. "You're Lisa's sister."

"Seth, I—"

The office door opened, and the information officer poked his head in. "Hey, there, Seth." He glanced at her. "Just checking to be sure you found everything you wanted."

"Yes." She forced herself to smile, forced her voice to hold steady. She'd gotten much more than she wanted, but it was probably just what she deserved.

"Anything else I can do for you?" He was relentlessly cheery.

"No, thanks." She clicked out of the personnel program. "I'm all finished."

He glanced from her to Seth, seemed to register that he wasn't needed, and backed out with a wave.

"We can't talk here."

"No." The shock was gone from his eyes now, replaced by anger and determination. "Not here, but we *are* going to talk."

She tried to think. "I can meet you later." Even an hour or so might give her time to marshal her thoughts and find a way to explain the unexplainable.

"Not later." Seth's voice was implacable. "Now."

"All right." She really didn't have any bargaining space. "Where?"

"Your hotel."

"No." She didn't have to think twice about not wanting to be closed in with him.

He shook his head, annoyed. "All right, then. The

park, where we took Davy that day. We can have a private conversation there."

She nodded. "My car is in the parking lot."

"So is mine. I'll follow you there."

He obviously didn't intend to let her out of his sight until he had the answers he wanted. Well, she couldn't blame him for that.

She swept her things into her bag with icy fingers and got up. Seth held the door open for her, like a jailer ushering a prisoner from a cell to the court.

It took an effort to walk steadily past him, to feel him moving close behind her as she started down the hallway. Her mind scrambled this way and that, but she didn't see any way out.

Seth wanted the truth, and this time nothing else would do. A shiver went down her spine. Telling him the truth would bring him into contact with her father, and she couldn't begin to guess what trouble that might cause.

Seth stayed right on the bumper of Julie's rental car through afternoon traffic. Horns blared when he cut someone off, but he ignored them. He wasn't going to lose her now, not until he had some answers.

Actually, she didn't seem to be trying to make a break for it. She drove cautiously, almost too cautiously, stopping for every yellow light.

All he wanted was to get there.

The silver rental car stopped at yet another light, and he slammed the steering wheel in frustration. The anger that pounded through him was foreign to him, and he didn't know what to do with it.

He didn't react that way. Ask anyone. He listened; he watched; he offered advice if asked for it. He tried to help. That's who he was.

Not this time. This time it was personal. This time it involved his son. His heart lurched at the thought of Davy. He'd do anything, take on anyone, to protect his son.

Julie was Davy's aunt. He tried to get his mind around that fact. Did that mean she had rights where Davy was concerned? He didn't know, and he didn't think he wanted to find out.

Her turn signal blinked, and she made the right onto Park Street. He followed her. In a moment they'd be there. He'd get answers. Why was she here? What about the private detective she claimed her father hired?

Why had she lied about who she was to all of them?

That was the bottom line. If Julie didn't have anything to hide, why would she lie?

She pulled into a parking space, and he drew in right behind her. There'd be no sympathy or softness for Julie until she told him the truth.

She met him on the sidewalk, keeping a careful distance between them, and her eyes evaded his.

"Over there." He gestured toward a bench under a maple tree. It was far enough from the play area that no one was likely to come near them.

Julie nodded and started across the grass. He strode

along beside her. He'd hold his tongue until they were seated. He wanted to be able to see Julie's face when she tried to talk her way out of this.

She sank to the bench as if with relief, and he sat down next to her, angling his body so that he faced her. So that he could study her.

Julie's face was still pale against the soft blue shirt she wore under her suede jacket, but not as blanched as it had been in the office. He'd thought she was going to pass out for a moment there. She still bore lines of strain around her eyes that made her look older.

"Okay," he said abruptly. He wasn't going to start feeling sorry for her after what she'd done. "Let's start at the beginning. Why did you come here?"

"I came because I'd found out my sister was dead." She met his eyes then, something stiffening in her. "I know you have plenty of reason to be angry with me, but you share some of the blame. You didn't even let me know that my sister had died."

She'd gone on the offensive, and he hadn't expected that. He had to slow down, take a breath, figure out how to deal with this.

"I didn't let you know because I didn't know who you were. I knew Lisa had a sister. I knew she was estranged from her family. That was it."

"Lisa didn't even tell you her family's name?"

He heard the doubt in her voice. "She didn't tell, and I didn't ask." Maybe he should have, but he'd never wanted to push on what was obviously a painful spot.

"You could have found us, if you'd wanted to."

His anger spurted up again. "I could have, but I knew that wasn't what Lisa wanted. She'd made her feelings quite clear. She never wanted to see any of you again."

Julie winced as if he'd hit her, and he felt a flicker of shame. Maybe he shouldn't have been so blunt, but she'd asked for it.

"You didn't think that we should have been told of her death." She said the words evenly, but he could hear pain beneath them.

He took a breath, shaking his head. "Okay, maybe I was letting my grief run things at first. My parents thought I should try to notify Lisa's family, but all I wanted to do was follow her wishes."

Her mouth trembled, and she pressed her lips together. "I don't know about my father, but I would have come."

To Lisa's funeral. The words were implied, but they brought back a flood of memories of that terrible day. Grief. Guilt. The emotions roiled through him again.

"That's what I decided," he said shortly. "Later, I figured if her family ever wanted anything to do with Lisa, they'd have shown up at some point. They never did. Until now."

"Yes." She looked down at her hands, the fingers twisting together in her lap.

"How did you find out?"

She glanced up, as if relieved at the question. "Our

aunt had left some money in trust for Lisa, and I was the administrator. The fund was accumulating, and I wanted to find out what she wanted done with it."

"She never spoke of it to me. She probably didn't want it."

"Maybe not, but it was my duty to take care of it for her. My search led me to the fact that my sister was dead. And that she'd left a child."

"You hadn't tried to reach her in years. Why should you suddenly care?"

She squeezed her eyes closed for an instant. "At the very least, because Davy is her son. He's entitled to her share of the estate."

His guard went up at the mention of Davy. "I don't want any money from you."

"It's not mine, it's Lisa's. According to the terms of the trust, it reverts to Davy."

"I still don't want it. My son has everything he needs."

"He's my sister's son, too." Tears sparkled suddenly in her green eyes. "Can't you understand that I wanted to see him?"

Presumably even the coldhearted family Lisa had described might want to see her son or shed a tear at her grave.

"Okay, I can accept that. But that doesn't explain why you lied about who you are."

"I just—" She stopped, seeming to gather her thoughts. "Look, I know you can't understand. Lisa didn't want anything to do with us for good reason. I thought if I told you who I was, you might refuse to talk with me. You might not let me see Davy."

He couldn't honestly say he knew how he'd have reacted. He would hope he could have been fair to her, but he just didn't know.

He shook his head, trying to free himself from the doubts that cluttered his mind. "What about this supposed story of yours? Are you really a photographer? Does the magazine even exist or is that a figment of your imagination, too?"

A flush came up in her cheeks. "Of course I'm a photographer. You saw the magazine articles I brought to the house."

Apparently she could be touched on the subject of her profession, if nothing else. "That doesn't explain the story you were supposed to be writing."

"I thought about how I could approach you. How you might respond. I didn't know what Lisa had told you about me. So I decided to ask for help from an editor I often work with. She was pleased with the story idea."

"So you got in touch with the chief." She had a pretty devious mind to have figured all this out just to get near his family.

"He wanted the publicity the article would give the department. It wasn't difficult to make sure he assigned you to help me."

"And the story? Did you ever intend for it to see the light of day?"

That flush touched her cheeks again. "I'd like it to. I guess at this point it depends on you."

He couldn't even consider that now. "You used it to get close to me. You used me to get close to my son."

The thought of that deception burned. He hadn't just been fooled. He'd been attracted. He'd kissed her. He'd trusted her.

"I just wanted to be sure Davy was all right." She clenched her hands tightly in her lap. "I thought I could assess the situation from the outside, figure out if he needed anything. Decide how best to handle the trust."

"You could have done that without lying to us." *To me, Julie. You lied to me when you kissed me.*

"I thought it was best to do it without getting emotionally involved."

He raised his eyebrows. "Are you cold enough to do that?"

"No." Shame and regret mingled in her face. "I'm not."

He thought that was the truest thing she'd said. He wasn't ready to forgive her, not by a long shot. But he could accept that she was hurting, too.

"What about your father? Was he in on this?"

"No. I didn't tell him. This is why I had to keep it a secret."

Suspicion flared. "You said he hired the private investigator. You'd better try harder to keep your stories straight."

Those soft lips of hers tightened to a thin line. "I didn't tell him, but he found out. He hired the investigator. I didn't know anything about it until Brendan and Claire found out who he was."

This was like fighting his way through a smoky fire, not knowing which way was up. "You know about it now. Why did he do that? What's he after?"

Her gaze slid away from his. "He told me that he wanted the same thing I did. To be sure Davy was safe and happy and had everything he needed."

"Well, why didn't he just ask me? I might not like it, but I wouldn't have refused to speak with Davy's grandfather. Who is he, anyway?"

Julie stared at him, her eyes wide. "You really don't know who our father is?"

He moved impatiently. "Would I be asking if I knew?"

Julie tried to think this through rationally. She'd assumed that at some point Lisa would have told Seth her father's identity, even though she'd made it clear she didn't want to have anything to do with him.

But Seth hadn't known. Was it going to make a difference in his attitude when he found out?

She watched him, intent on his reaction. "Our father is Ronald Phillip Alexander."

He frowned. "Ronald Alexander? Are you talking about the Ronald Alexander who's supposed to be one of the richest men in Maryland?"

"The sixth richest, according to the last article I read that compared things like that."

Seth's face hardened. "I don't care how rich the man is. Why didn't he just come to me if he wanted to know something about Davy? Why did he hire a private investigator? Is that how you people deal with family?"

"There's no 'you people' about it." She managed a little tartness in her voice at that. "Please don't classify me with him. I lead my own life, and I don't depend on Alexander money to do it."

"I remember what you said about your family." His gaze probed. "Was that the truth?"

Small wonder that he questioned everything she'd said to him. "Yes. I just didn't say that there'd been a daughter of that second marriage. Lisa."

He looked at her steadily. "I'll try and believe that, Julie. But I still want to know why he hired a private investigator."

"I talked to him over the weekend. That was why I went back to Baltimore after I found out about the detective."

"Not to see your editor."

"No." He was probably counting up the lies she'd told. "I talked with my father. He told me that he didn't want to interfere in Davy's life. He just wants to be sure he's all right, and to get enough information to set up a trust for Davy in his will."

She thought about the rest of what he'd said—that he didn't want the Flanagans coming to him for money. He didn't know them.

"Look, I don't know how many times I have to say it. I don't want anything from him, and Davy doesn't need anything. I can take care of my son."

Her fingers were numb from clenching them so

tightly. "It may not be that easy. He seems very deter-mined. He asked me—" She'd like those words back, but it was too late.

"He asked you what?"

"He agreed to call off the private investigator if I'd take care of getting the information for him."

"That's what you were doing today. Checking my personnel records so you could run to him with them." The wave of anger that came from him was so hot it was a wonder it didn't scorch the bench.

"You have every right to be angry. I wouldn't have agreed to do it, but he'd just have sent another investi-gator if I hadn't." She hesitated, trying to be sure she wasn't making excuses. "I hope that's why I agreed. I still find it difficult to say no to him."

"That's funny, because it doesn't bother me at all. I guess I'd better tell him myself to stay out of our lives."

"Don't do that." She hadn't known how much she feared that outcome until he said it. "Please. Don't start a battle with him."

His jaw hardened. "I'm not looking to go to battle. He's Lisa's father, after all. Surely it's possible to have a civil conversation with him and point out politely that he wasn't part of his daughter's world while she was alive, and it's too late to mend that now."

Something inside her shuddered at the thought of Seth heading into a confrontation with her father and getting mauled in the process.

"Please, don't." She leaned toward him, wanting to

touch him but not daring to. "I know you don't have any reason to trust me, but believe me when I say that you don't want to make an enemy of my father."

"I'm not afraid of him, Julie. It's pretty clear that you and Lisa were, but I'm not."

She squeezed her eyes shut for an instant against the pain that swept over her. "You've never dealt with anyone like him before."

"You mean an ordinary firefighter doesn't know how to mix with the rich and famous."

"No." She hoped he could read the sincerity in her eyes. "I mean that you're an honest, honorable man. And he's a powerful, devious one. I don't want you to get hurt. More importantly, I don't want Davy to get hurt."

Probably only the mention of Davy made him pause. "All right. What do you suggest?"

"Please, just let me deal with him. He doesn't ever have to know that we had this conversation. With a little luck, you'll never hear from him again. If he leaves money to Davy, you can put it in the bank and ignore it until he's old enough to know about it."

Please.

Seth surged to his feet, as if he couldn't be still any longer. Took a step away from her, then swung back. She could see the battle that raged inside him. A lot of that anger was still directed at her, obviously. How could it be otherwise?

I told myself I was doing what was best for Davy,

Lord. I just succeeded in hurting everyone, and I don't know how to make this right.

"I'll think about it," Seth said. "I'll talk it over with the family. Unlike your family, we actually talk to each other."

She couldn't say anything to that. It was true.

"All right." She stood, trying to make it sound as if this were any goodbye. "I'll stay at the hotel until I hear from you."

He gave a curt nod. "I'll get back to you. But understand this, Julie. I'm not going to let anyone interfere with the way I raise my son. If you can't tell your father that, I will."

Chapter Thirteen

Julie pulled the rental car to the curb in front of the Flanagan house the next night, her fingers cold when she switched off the ignition. She'd spent twenty-four hours cooped up in her hotel room, waiting for something to happen. For Seth to call, or for her father to call, or for a band of Flanagans to turn up with tar and feathers.

Finally Seth had phoned. His voice had been cool and businesslike, giving nothing away. He'd asked her to come to the house tonight to meet with the family. The trouble was, they'd both known this call wasn't an invitation. It was a summons.

Please, Lord. She gripped the steering wheel with both hands. *I know I've messed up everything. I was wrong to go into this by trying to deceive them, no matter how good I thought my reasons were. Please show me a way to help them. Please forgive me.*

If they wouldn't listen to her, if Seth insisted on confronting her father, she didn't know what would happen. She just knew it would be bad.

She slid out of the car, tugging her jacket down, hoping she could manage to look calm and collected in front of Seth's family, no matter what they said. Probably the best she could expect was that she'd manage to save her tears for later, when she was alone.

The light that poured from the windows didn't look welcoming now, and the curving walk was too short. It got her to the front door too fast.

She stopped at the top of the stairs, her fingers clenching the strap of her handbag. She didn't have her camera to hide behind tonight. She had to face people who had every reason to hate her.

Her finger was still on the doorbell when Seth opened the door. Silhouetted against the light behind him, he was a tall, ominous figure. She could read nothing of his expression.

"Julie. Come in."

She nodded, trying to swallow the lump in her throat, and stepped inside. This was going to hurt, and there was no way around it.

Brendan, Ryan and Terry sat next to each other on the sofa. Seth's parents occupied their usual chairs. Only Gabe and Mary Kate were missing. She struggled to steel herself against the antagonistic glances sent her way. The Flanagans were lined up like a jury ready to convict.

Seth gestured to a chair that had been set to face the

others. The defendant's seat, she supposed. She sat down, her bag dropping to the floor from nerveless fingers.

Seth went to lean against the fireplace, as if he couldn't relax enough to sit down. The glance he turned on her was one he'd turn on a stranger.

No, that was wrong. He'd be friendly to a stranger, with that open, easy grin that lit his eyes. He looked at her as if she were an enemy.

"I've told the family what I found out from you yesterday." No more secrets, he seemed to be saying. "We thought we'd better clear things up with you."

"There's plenty to clear up." Terry's voice was edgy and antagonistic. The camaraderie they'd shared at the fire was gone.

Brendan touched Terry's arm, and she subsided.

Obviously they'd planned this for when Davy was in bed. Would she ever see him again? Her heart splintered. They had the power to shut her off from him forever.

She'd better say what she had to as quickly as possible, while she could.

"I'd like to begin by apologizing to you." Her voice sounded steadier than she'd have thought possible, given the fact that pain had a stranglehold on her throat. "I'm sorry that I deceived you about who I am and why I was here. You've been nothing but kind to me and you didn't deserve to be treated that way."

Joe leaned forward, hands on his knees, his square face set. "Seth told us what you said, but I still don't get why you didn't just tell us who you are. We wouldn't have tried to keep you from seeing Davy."

"I know that now. I didn't then." She swallowed. How could she explain a family like hers to them? "Lisa had made it clear that she didn't want any contact with her family, but when I learned about her death, I felt I had to be sure her son was all right."

Siobhan glanced at Seth. "We should have gotten in touch with Lisa's people at the time Lisa died. I knew it wasn't right."

"I can understand why you didn't." She didn't look at Seth, because she didn't want to see the dislike in his eyes. "Lisa felt that cutting ties with her family completely was the only way she could make a life for herself, and Seth wanted to respect that. Maybe she was right."

"So you thought you'd come and see that Davy was okay." Brendan's voice was carefully neutral. "Then what were you going to do?"

"Disappear." That was an easy answer, although it had proved impossible to do. "That seemed best. I'd have tried to figure out a way to ensure Davy had the income from his mother's trust, but I didn't intend to make myself known to you."

"Why not?" Ryan shot the words at her, his expressive eyes showing contempt. "Afraid we'd hit you up for a loan?"

It was close enough to what her father had said to give her pause. "No. I just thought it would be better— safer—if my father didn't know anything about Davy."

"I don't understand." Siobhan looked distressed. "He's Davy's grandfather, even if he and Lisa never got along. We wouldn't try to keep him from seeing Davy."

She didn't know how to explain Ronald Alexander to someone like Siobhan—someone who created a home filled with love and happiness for anyone who walked through the door. This place must have seemed like heaven to Lisa.

"My father is not a kind person," she said carefully. "I was afraid that if he knew about Davy, he'd try to interfere in his life."

Seth shifted his weight on the balls of his feet, as if preparing for a fight. "I'm Davy's father. There's nothing he can do."

"I wish I could agree with that, but I can't." She had to make Seth understand the danger. "I've seen my father wield power. Maybe he couldn't actually take Davy away from you, but he can afford all the high-powered lawyers in the state if he wants. He could make your lives miserable."

Ryan shot to his feet. "That's crazy. Just because you and Lisa were afraid of him, you think everyone should be." He glared at her. "He can't do anything to us."

She wouldn't let herself rub the throbbing that had begun in her temples, because it would be a sign of weakness.

"You've already had a little taste of it, with the private investigator looking into Seth's life. That wasn't pleasant, was it?"

"I can put up with it." Seth's voice was curt. "I'm not afraid of your father."

"Maybe you should be." The support came, unexpectedly, from Joe. His ruddy face darkened. "I've seen plenty of dirty tricks in my time. It's a bad combination for a man to have lots of money and no sense of shame."

Joe had put his finger on it exactly, without ever having met her father. Ronald Alexander had no sense of shame. He did what suited him, without regard for whether it was right or wrong, only whether it was against the law.

"Even it that's true, Dad, what do you expect me to do?" Seth looked baffled and angry. "I can't wait around for the man to cause trouble for my son. I should go and see him."

She took a long breath, trying to relax her throat enough to speak evenly. "I realize you don't want to take my word for anything, but I believe it would be a mistake to confront him. Right now, he says he just wants to know enough about the situation to make proper provision for Davy in his will. If you see him, especially if you get his back up, he's capable of causing trouble just because—well, because that's how he is."

She'd never been able to understand what made her father the person he was. She probably never would.

Ryan gave a short laugh. "Maybe you should listen to her, Seth. It sounds like he could make even you angry."

"So what are you suggesting, Julie?" Siobhan looked at her gravely, her eyes seeming to stare right to her soul.

They seemed to be softening. Now was her chance. *Please, Lord, make them listen.*

"I think I should stay in Suffolk a few more days, sending my father the reports he asked for. If he meant what he said about not interfering, he'll rewrite his will and that should be the end of it. You won't have to worry about us any longer."

I'll go out of your life, Seth. I know that's what you want.

Seth frowned. "I don't like to do nothing."

"We won't," Joe said. "We'll get a lawyer lined up, just in case we need one. But if doing it Julie's way avoids a fight, so much the better." He glanced around the room from face to face. "Well?"

One after the other, they nodded.

Apparently they had an agreement. She stood, wanting nothing more than to be out of there before the weight of her pain crashed down on her. "I'll let you know anything I hear from him."

"You'd better." Seth's tone was implacable. "If your way doesn't work, we'll deal with him ourselves."

He would. He didn't realize he'd be David going up against Goliath, but without even a slingshot.

She nodded, turning toward the door. Maybe, if she went quickly, she could reach the car before she fell apart. She grasped the doorknob.

"Julie." Siobhan's voice stopped her with her hand

still on the knob, her throat thick with unshed tears. "You said you were going to disappear as soon as you knew Davy was all right. Why didn't you?"

Honesty compelled her to look at the woman she would have liked to have called a friend.

"I couldn't." Tears flooded her eyes, and she tried futilely to blink them back. "You must know why. I loved him the moment I saw him."

She spun away from them, yanked the door open and ran for the car.

"Well, what do you think?"

Seth leaned against the kitchen counter, watching his mother's face. In the hour since Julie had run out of the house, his mother had said very little. While the rest of them went back and forth over every word that had been said, Mom had turned inward. Praying, maybe.

She rinsed a cup slowly, put it in the rack and then turned to look at him. "I was thinking about those two girls."

For an instant he didn't understand. "You mean Lisa and Julie." Coupling their names felt odd. He hadn't been thinking of them as siblings, like him and Ryan.

"Their childhood must have been a bitter thing, to damage both of them so much."

Damage them. His mind grappled with the thought.

"What do you mean? Lisa—well, she didn't want to have anything to do with them, but she was okay."

Wasn't she? "And Julie—she's successful. Rich, I guess."

Her loving eyes studied his face. "It seems to me they both carried scars from their childhood."

He moved, trying to ease the discomfort from his soul. "It's not as if he beat them."

"There are worse things you can do to a child than hit them. Make them feel unloved, for example. Make them feel unworthy of ever being loved."

Something cold settled deep inside him. Was that why Lisa had never been able to find happiness, even with a husband and a baby?

His mother polished the counter with a cloth, not looking at him. "You know, I have to admire Julie."

"Admire her?" His mother frequently surprised him with the breadth of her ability to love, but this seemed a reach even for her. "After what she did?"

"She was wrong to lie to us and she certainly went about things the wrong way. But look at her efforts on Davy's behalf. She hadn't even known he existed until recently."

"She definitely went the wrong way." He'd been trying not to think of those kisses they'd shared. Had that been all part of the act?

"And she has courage, at least. She didn't run away from her troubles, even though it might have been easier."

"She still lied to us." The thought hardened in him. "I can't forgive that."

"Don't say that, son." Siobhan put her hand on his

arm. "Don't ever close your heart to forgiveness. It will hurt you far more than the other person."

His mouth curved in an involuntary smile, and he leaned over to press a kiss against her soft cheek. "You are one great mother. Have I mentioned that lately?"

"Not often enough." She patted his cheek. "Actually, there are a couple of things I have to thank Julie for, in spite of her deceit."

He lifted an eyebrow, prepared to be surprised. "What?"

"Well, you're not talking about making a foolish marriage for companionship any more, are you?"

He winced. "I guess not." Not after what he'd begun to feel for Julie. Companionship seemed pretty tepid after that.

"And then there are the photographs. We'd never get pictures like that of Davy. We've got the love, but not the skill. Julie has both."

"If you're saying I should forgive her just because she says she loves Davy—"

"Not says. She doesn't have to say. It's clear in every picture she took."

"Even so."

She shrugged, turning away. "I was just thinking about how hurt and lonely Julie must be feeling about now. It seems to me a person who's trying to do the right thing doesn't deserve that."

Julie had taken a hot shower, changed into her most comfortable sweat suit and downed a cup of hot tea.

Now she curled up on the loveseat in the tiny living room of her suite, trying to get warm. Even the blanket she'd pulled over her didn't help.

She'd never felt as cold as she had when Seth stared at her the way he had. Oh, he couldn't be cruel, as her father had been. Seth didn't have it in him to be cruel.

But still, that look had sliced her heart into pieces. It would be far better for her if she never saw him again.

She pressed her fingers to her temples, trying to look at this situation rationally. She'd told Seth he was a buffer and he hadn't denied it. Now she was the one trying to be a buffer. Trying to protect him, even though he didn't think he either wanted or needed that protection.

But Davy did. Her heart clutched at the thought of Davy's bright, beautiful confidence. It came from never having doubted that he was loved and cherished.

Would that be enough to protect him if he had to enter into a relationship with her father? Or would it be nipped by the frost of his icy disapproval?

A knock at the door startled her. She tossed the blanket onto the back of the loveseat and went to open it.

Seth. Seth stood there. She tried to steel herself. Whatever he wanted, she had to deal with it.

She took the chain off and opened the door wide. "Do you need something more?"

"No." He came in, studying her face as if he could read the traces of the futile tears she'd shed. "I came to see if you're all right."

The unexpected kindness made her eyes well with tears.

"I'm—" She wanted to say that she was fine, but the words wouldn't come out. They stuck in her throat, choking her.

He shouldn't be looking at her with concern on his face. She didn't deserve it. She couldn't deal with it.

She shook her head, turning away from him, struggling to regain her composure. His hands came down on her shoulders, warm and strong.

"I'm sorry." His voice went low and soft. "I shouldn't have been so hard on you."

That softness undermined whatever was left of her control. She tried to take a breath, but it came out as a sob.

Seth gave a murmured, incoherent sound of distress. Then he drew her onto the loveseat, sat down next to her and pulled her into the comfort of his arms.

She couldn't stop the tears. If he'd been cold and angry, she'd have found the strength, but his kindness opened the floodgates. The sobs ripped through her.

Seth didn't do anything. He didn't say anything but the kind of soft, reassuring phrases she'd heard him say to Davy the night he'd been ill. She'd never known such comfort. She never wanted it to end.

But it had to. She pulled away finally, trying to regain control.

"Sorry." The word came out on a hiccup, and her throat felt too raw to try again. Her eyes burned from the tears.

Seth rubbed his hand soothingly along her arm. "Don't keep saying you're sorry. Everyone's got a right to fall apart now and then. You don't have to apologize for that."

She pressed her palms to her eyes and took a deep breath. "In my family you did. It was considered inappropriate to lose control of yourself."

She remembered, only too well, stammering out an apology in the face of that cold-eyed stare that made her feel as if she were defective.

He took her hands in his and held them warmly. "Listen, you don't have to run your life by your father's rules any longer. You're trying to do the right thing. That's what's important."

"Are you sure?" She studied his face, longing to believe he meant that. "That's not the impression I got from you a couple of hours ago."

He smoothed her fingers. "My mother pointed out how dumb I was being."

"I'm sure Siobhan didn't say any such thing."

He smiled. "Not in so many words, no. But she pointed out that you were already hurting, and it wasn't fair to keep kicking you."

She blinked away the tears that threatened to recur. "Your mother is very kind. And very wise."

"Tell me about it. She said something that made me think." He hesitated, his brows drawing down. "She said that you and Lisa had both been damaged by your childhood. I guess I hadn't thought about it that way."

She looked down at their intertwined hands. His

were strong and wiry, and there was a pale scar across the back of the right one. They were capable hands that could put out a fire or comfort a child.

"I suppose that's true. Lisa and I didn't know that all families weren't like ours. We thought that we were the ones at fault. That we didn't measure up."

"What about your mother? Lisa's mother?"

"I don't remember my mother at all. I remember Lisa's mother a little." A whiff of some expensive perfume, the rustle of silk. "Sometimes she'd come in to say good-night to us. They both left."

"Neither of them tried to gain custody of you?"

"Not that I know of. They just went out of our lives. We knew we weren't supposed to ask about them. It would have made Father angry."

His fingers tightened. "He hurt you?"

"Not physically. He'd never do that. I don't think he ever touched us at all."

"No hugs?"

"No hugs." She thought of the easy, casual hugs the Flanagans seemed to exchange on every occasion. Of the way Davy raced to be hugged, always sure of being caught, embraced, tossed into the air. "Not like your family."

His smile flickered. "Everyone's not like us."

"He just—disapproved." She shook her head. "I don't think I can explain the power of that feeling. He has a way of looking at you as if you're a piece of shoddy merchandise he's considering returning to the store."

He pulled her back against his shoulder. "There's nothing shoddy about you. The man sounds like an idiot."

She shouldn't lean on him this way. "He's not that. Your father had it right, I think. All that matters to him is what he wants. He wanted perfect daughters who would be a lovely reflection on him. Neither Lisa nor I ever measured up to that, and he let us know it. I remember—"

"What do you remember?" He prodded when she stopped.

"There was a boy, when I was in college. I thought I was in love with him. More to the point, I thought he was in love with me."

"What happened?"

"My father found out that he'd been taking pictures of me, trying to peddle a story to the tabloids. 'Poor little rich girl' kind of thing." The taste of it was still acid in her mouth after all these years.

"What did your father do?"

"Bought him off. And pointed out to me that it was highly unlikely anyone would be interested in me for any other reason." She shook her head. "Sorry. That really sounds self-pitying. I came to know, eventually, that I was valuable in God's sight. That's what matters."

"I guess I can see now why Lisa ran away."

"Yes." Her throat went tight. "She ran away when she was in high school, but the police brought her back. After that she waited. Once she was in college, she planned to disappear. She said it was the only way she could have a life of her own. So she did. She was braver than I was."

He stroked her back, as if he felt her pain. "You didn't know where she was all that time?"

"I should have." The guilt pulled at her. "I should have tried to find her. When she was little, I promised to take care of her. I didn't do it."

He was still for a moment. "I promised to take care of her, too. And I failed."

"You didn't know." Her voice choked. "You didn't know what you were up against. I did."

Seth took her face between his hands, looking into her eyes with a gravity she'd never seen before.

"Listen to me, Julie. This is not your fault. You weren't responsible for what happened to Lisa. You were a child yourself. Someone should have been taking care of you."

She'd have liked to believe that, but she couldn't. "I can't absolve myself that easily. I was the big sister. But if I can help keep Davy safe, maybe I can make up for that."

And if she couldn't—

Seth didn't see the extent of the danger. She did.

Chapter Fourteen

Two days later, Julie sat staring at the laptop she'd put on the scarred tabletop in the firehouse kitchen. The crew had gone out on a call, but no one had suggested that she go with them. She seemed to be existing in a kind of armed truce with the firefighters.

So why was she still working on the article? It was highly unlikely the piece would ever appear in print.

Still, writing the article had helped to keep her sane for the past couple of days. She'd felt as if she were in limbo since the evening she'd wept in Seth's arms.

She'd been closer to him in those moments than she ever had to another human being, except possibly Lisa. Seth had felt that closeness, too—she was sure of it.

But then they'd both drawn back, seeing the danger. Maybe what she recognized in Seth was the thing she'd begun to recognize in herself—an inability to open the heart to a deep emotional connection.

They had different reasons for that failing. With Seth it was a matter of personality, as far as she could tell. Maybe because of his position in the middle of a large family, he'd adopted the role of everyone's friend. He seemed to prefer being the observer or the peacemaker rather than participating in the fray.

She put her palms over her eyes, staring into the darkness for a moment, as if that would help her see more clearly. Her situation was different. Her heart had been bruised so thoroughly, at such a tender age, that she wasn't sure about how it would function in the future. Or if she even had the courage to try to change.

Lord, I've had to face some painful things about myself during my time here. Maybe that was always Your plan.

She had made some moves toward risking her heart, hadn't she? Her heart had opened a little to the Flanagans, more to Davy, still more to Seth. She just didn't know if she could go further.

Well, Seth might not want that, in any event. Their situation was so complex. Why on earth would someone like Seth want to risk the painful complications of a relationship with her when he so obviously preferred things emotionally smooth and easy?

The rumble of the truck coming into the garage warned her that the crew was back. Apparatus, she reminded herself, not truck. They never referred to it as a truck. She was learning some firefighter lingo, anyway, whether she ever used it in the article or not.

Footsteps sounded on the stairs and laughing voices echoed in the stairwell. Something inside her relaxed. The call couldn't have been a serious one or they wouldn't sound like that.

They trooped into the kitchen, saw her there, and the easy laughter stopped. She wasn't one of the gang anymore. That hurt more than she'd have expected.

She arranged a smile on her face. "So, was it an easy call?"

Dave smiled back at her, the look a little wary but at least not openly antagonistic. "It was if you can call it easy when Ryan has to go down into a storm drain after a stuck kitten."

"I still say it would have come out by itself if they'd put out a can of cat food," Ryan grumbled.

"Yeah, but then we wouldn't have had the fun of watching you." Seth clapped him on the back. "Go take a shower, will you?"

They scattered, with Ryan moving off toward the crew quarters and the others going back down to the garage. Either accidentally or on purpose, they left her and Seth alone.

He looked as if he'd like to follow the others, but something held him in place. He wandered to the counter and poured a mug of coffee.

She had to say something to break the uncomfortable silence. "I sent that information we agreed on to my father." She closed the computer. "I haven't heard anything more from him."

Seth nodded, frowning. He leaned back against the

counter. It was his usual easy pose, but she detected tension in the long lines of his body.

Her own tension edged up in response. What was bothering him? He clearly intended to say something to her.

He set the mug down on the counter, as if he didn't want the coffee after all. "I thought you should know," he said abruptly. "I've decided to take that promotion."

She blinked, her mind readjusting to the unexpected subject. "You have? Why?" And why was he telling her?

He shoved himself away from the counter and planted his hands on the back of the wooden chair next to her. He was close enough that her breath caught.

"I decided you were right. It's better for Davy if I accept the promotion." He frowned down at her.

"You don't look very happy about it."

He held the frown for a moment longer. Then he shrugged, some of the tension easing from his shoulders. He pulled out the chair and sat down.

"I guess I am still fighting it a bit," he admitted. "But the decision's made. I turned in the paperwork to the chief this morning."

"And you decided this why, exactly?" She was feeling her way, not sure what this turn of events meant. "In what way was I right about the promotion?"

Seth planted his elbows on the table, folding his hands loosely in front of him. "Davy doesn't have a mother. I owe it to him to take a position that might be a bit safer."

She considered that. "Did you make this decision because of my father?"

"I figure it can't hurt," he said. "Maybe being a lieutenant will make me a bit more of a solid citizen in his eyes."

At least he seemed to be taking her concerns about her father seriously. She was relieved. Perhaps the emotional meltdown she'd had that night had made him think about the gravity of the situation.

"But you don't really want to be a lieutenant."

She wanted to know more—to know how he felt inside about the move he'd committed to. He'd sacrifice anything for Davy—she knew that without asking.

He shrugged. "It's not a big deal. If it makes things easier for my son, that's a small price to pay."

He'd said exactly what she was thinking. "You'll be a good lieutenant."

"Maybe." He turned toward her a little. "I guess everything that's happened lately has kind of pushed me out of my comfort zone."

Like holding me while I cried, Seth? Did that push you out of your comfort zone?

"So this is just another step in that direction."

"I guess." For a moment he stared down at his hands. Then he swung to face her, his eyes serious, warming when they rested on her. "Okay, I'm hedging. That's not all of it."

Her heart started to thud at the look in his face, and her breath caught.

"What is?" Her voice sounded breathless.

"You." His fingers closed over hers, sending impulses racing along her nerves and straight to her heart. "I don't know why, Julie. But when you tell me I make a good leader, I start believing it."

She shouldn't let his words, his touch, affect her so strongly. "The others think so, too." It came out in a whisper.

"I don't care about that." His grip tightened. "I care about what you think."

That wasn't the same as saying he cared about her, but it was close enough to make her heart race. To make her yearn to tell him what she felt. His gaze was intent on her face, and she felt as if she were falling into the depths of that look.

"Seth, I—"

"Hey, Seth." Dave's voice echoed up the stairwell. "There's a guy here looking for you."

Seth drew back, blinking as if he were confused. He shook his head and then pushed his chair back, standing.

"Okay," he called back. "Send him up."

He glanced at her. "Sorry," he said softly.

She nodded, trying to smile. Was he sorry for the interruption? Or sorry for what had almost happened?

Maybe this visitor, whoever he was, had better timing than he'd have imagined. Seth gripped the back on the chair with one hand, not letting himself look at Julie. He didn't want to see what might be in her eyes.

He'd been on dangerous ground there for a moment, with flames closing in around him on all sides. He'd almost succumbed to the feelings that raged inside him.

Back up, he ordered himself. Anyone with an ounce of sense would say that a relationship between him and Julie would be a disaster. He knew that. She undoubtedly did, too.

Still, he couldn't help longing.

The man who emerged at the top of the steps was young, with a quick, curious glance that took in the whole area before focusing on him. "Are you Seth Flanagan?"

He hadn't seen the guy before, he was sure of that. "That's me."

"Glad to meet you." He held out his right hand, and Seth extended his automatically.

The man slapped a paper into it, then skipped nimbly toward the stairs. "Consider yourself served."

"What?" He stared blankly at the folded paper in his hand, and then he took a quick step after the guy. "What is all this?"

But it was too late. He was gone, clattering down the steps and out the door in a moment.

"What is it?" Apprehension colored Julie's voice. She moved to stand next to him. "What did he give you?"

He unfolded the paper, unable to prevent the sense of dread that settled heavily into him. For a long moment he stared at the words as if they'd been written in a language he didn't know. Slowly his brain began to make sense of them.

"Your father is taking me to court." He looked at Julie. "He's suing for custody of Davy."

The color drained from her face. He reached out to grab her before she could topple over, and any brief thought that she'd been a part of this vanished.

"No. No." Her voice was choked.

"You didn't know." He was sure of it. He just had to say it.

"I didn't know." Shock threaded the words. Then her gaze leapt to his face. "I didn't know, Seth."

Anger worked its way through his shock, flaming up to warm him, making his mind start to work again.

"He used you. You realize that, don't you? He used you to get information about us."

Her lips trembled for a moment. She pressed them together. "I've told you everything I knew about him and what he was doing."

"You didn't tell me he'd try to get custody." He had to strike out at someone for this, and she was the only one he could blame.

A flame of answering anger flickered in her eyes. "I'm the one who warned you about him, remember?"

"You're also the one who lied to us."

She drew back as if he'd hit her. "You can't think I had anything to do with this."

"No." He had to admit that. He knew her that well, at least. "But you're the one who convinced us not to take any action on your father's interest in Davy. And look what happened."

"I'm sorry." Grief moved in her eyes. "I believed

my father meant it when he said he only wanted Davy
to have his proper share of his estate. I shouldn't have.
I should have known."

"You believed. I believed. It doesn't matter now."
He slapped the paper down on the table. "All that matters is saving my son."

She pressed one hand to her temple. "An attorney.
You need a good attorney, right away. Your father said
he'd contact someone."

"He did." He yanked out his cell phone, frowning
at Julie. "I'm going to set up a meeting now. I can't
waste any more time doing nothing."

If that blow hurt her, she seemed determined not to
show it. "I'd like to be there."

"Why?" He had a quick, instinctive reaction to shut
her out, to keep this only in the family. They were the
people he trusted.

"I might be of use."

"How? What could you do?"

She straightened her shoulders, her eyes somber as
she met his gaze. She didn't flinch.

"I let my father deceive me once. It won't happen
again. I know his tactics. That could help your lawyer."

"You want me to believe you'd actually stand up
against him, if it came to that?"

He'd thought she was pale before. Now she was
dead white. The only thing alive in her face was the
passion in her eyes.

"I'll do whatever I have to do to save Davy. Including testifying against my father in a court of law."

Would she? He felt a flicker of pity for her. She might want to but still not be able to after the way her father had conditioned her to fear him.

He suppressed the pity. He couldn't think of anyone or anything right now but Davy.

"You might have to."

She nodded, the movement stiff and jerky. "I will."

Julie sat on the straight-backed chair in the attorney's office that afternoon, mentally contrasting this place with the hallowed precincts of Justin, Bradford and Bradford, her father's attorneys. This wasn't even as big as their foyer. Or as expensively furnished.

That wouldn't matter, of course, if Calvin Morton was competent. Unfortunately, she was beginning to think he wasn't.

Joe, Siobhan and Seth occupied the other seats in front of Morton's gray metal desk, listening intently to one cautious platitude after another.

"This whole thing is ridiculous, isn't it?" Siobhan's eyes sought reassurance. "No judge would take a child away from his own father, would he, Cal?"

Morton ran a hand over thinning dark hair, as if to be sure it stayed in place. "I'm sure Seth doesn't have anything to worry about."

"I've been served with a custody suit." Seth leaned forward, his body tense. "I'd call that something to worry about."

"Well, of course, I mean, it always pays to be careful." He shot a wary glance at Julie. "You never can be absolutely sure what might happen once you get into court. Maybe it would be better to come to some agreement with Mr. Alexander before that happens."

"How can you say that?" Seth looked ready to launch himself across the desk. "I'm not agreeing to anything that gives that man power over my son."

"Compromise is not giving up," Morton said. "Maybe he'd agree to just have the boy for a visit a few times a year."

"No agreement." Seth's voice was flat. "No compromise. We fight this."

"If you're sure that's really what you want…" Morton let that trail off uncertainly.

One thing she was sure of was that her father's attorneys could eat this man for breakfast. Family friend or not, Morton wasn't in the right league for this case, and he probably knew it.

"You might want to think about getting an attorney in Baltimore," she suggested. "I'm sure Mr. Morton would agree that since the case is being brought there, it would be good to have someone who knows the system."

Morton looked as if she'd just thrown him a lifeline. "That's an excellent suggestion, Ms. Alexander. Excellent."

Joe frowned. "How would we know who to hire? We don't know any big-shot lawyers in Baltimore."

"Perhaps I could help you find the right person." The Flanagans were going to need a barracuda of a litigator if this came to court, and several names flickered through her mind. "I've lived in the city most of my life."

"Good idea," Morton said quickly. Everything about his body language said he'd like to see this troublesome matter walk right out of his office. "I'm sure you'll find someone. Of course, you know it will be expensive."

"We'll handle it," Joe said shortly.

They didn't have any idea how expensive this could be. Her father's attorneys could drag this thing out until the Flanagans were drained dry.

Well, that wasn't going to happen. It would be a pleasure to use the money her father had settled on her to fight him on this.

"You'd better pass this along to whoever you get." Morton handed an envelope across the desk to Seth.

Seth took it warily. "What is it?"

"A subpoena. They're trying to get hold of your late wife's medical records."

The Flanagans just looked puzzled. They didn't understand. Cold settled into her heart. But she did.

"Why on earth would they want Lisa's medical records?" Siobhan leaned toward Morton, clearly expecting him to have answers. "This is about Davy. Lisa died almost three years ago."

"I'm sure it's nothing." Morton waved his hands as if to dismiss it. "Nothing at all. They can't expect to gain any advantage from those old records."

She didn't want to say it, but she had to. "I think I know what they're up to."

Siobhan shifted the puzzled gaze to her. Julie tried to keep her eyes on Siobhan. She didn't want to see the pain in Seth's eyes.

"They might hope to prove that Lisa wasn't properly treated after Davy was born." She tried to choose the words carefully. "That perhaps her condition led to her death."

"Condition? What condition?" Joe shot the question at her. "She had a little case of the baby blues, that's all. So what?"

"If they could prove that her postpartum depression wasn't treated—"

"She means they'll try to prove that Lisa killed herself." Seth's voice was harsher than she'd ever heard it. "That's it, isn't it, Julie? You think they'll say that I contributed to her death because I didn't see to it that she received the care that would have saved her life."

"That's nonsense," Siobhan said quickly. "You weren't to blame. Anyway, it was an accident."

Seth's gaze bored into Julie as if his mother hadn't spoken. As if they were the only two people in the room.

"That might be what they're trying to prove," she admitted. "We all know it's not true, but they could try to use it against you."

"Do we know it's not true?" His words seemed splintered from rock.

Her heart felt as if it were breaking into pieces. "Yes," she said. "You're not to blame for what happened to Lisa."

The words lay between them, stark and painful—
the words he'd spoken to her when he talked about
Lisa's death. When he'd blamed himself.

He stared at her, his eyes dark with pain. "Was
that part of the information you gave your father,
Julie?"

They both knew what he was talking about. No
one else needed to know.

"I didn't tell him anything about it." She wouldn't
beg him to believe her. She could only hope he knew
the truth when he heard it.

He held her eyes an instant longer. Then he gave a
curt nod. She could breathe again.

Seth turned to his parents. Maybe he'd already realized that Morton wasn't going to be any use to them.

"Julie can find us a good lawyer in the city. In the
meantime, I'm going to Baltimore. I'm going to see
Ronald Alexander for myself."

"No," Siobhan said quickly. "I don't think that's a
good idea at all, Seth. Let the lawyers handle it."

"Really, I wouldn't advise—" Morton's voice pe-
tered out.

"I have to." Seth stood. "Take care of Davy for
me."

She couldn't stop him. She also couldn't let him go
alone. Everything was over between them, but she
still couldn't stand safely back from this battle.

Somehow she had to find the courage to do what
she could for Davy, even if that meant defying her father. Even if it meant splitting with him forever.

"I'll go with you." She forced herself out of the chair, moving as slowly as if she were very old. "I'll go with you to see my father."

Chapter Fifteen

They'd been silent in the car most of the way to Baltimore. Dusk had fallen, and lights came on in the buildings they passed. The beltway was a long stream of double headlamps as people headed home or out for the evening.

Julie leaned her head back against the headrest and watched Seth's hands on the steering wheel. He had to be tense, but it didn't show in his driving. He did that the way he did everything—competently, safely. One would always feel safe in his hands.

No. She turned her mind away from that painful thought. She couldn't think about being a part of Seth's life, because it wasn't going to happen. Too much pain lay between them to allow that.

Perhaps Seth felt as numb as she did right now. That was why she hadn't spoken. She couldn't make her mind work enough to form any words except for the most elemental prayer.

Please, Lord. Please, Lord. Davy is Your precious child. Show us how to protect him.

She leaned forward, her stomach cramping. "Take the next exit off to the right."

He nodded. "Thanks." He glanced toward her. "And thanks for coming with me."

"I'm not sure how much good I can do, but I'll try."

She couldn't let Seth go into this alone. She clung to that truth. No matter what else she could or couldn't do, she would be with him when he confronted her father.

They turned onto the wide avenue that announced they'd moved into one of the oldest and richest of Baltimore's suburbs. Seth let out a low whistle as they drove down the curving street.

"Pretty fancy neighborhood."

Through wrought-iron gates, Julie glimpsed a pink-and-white Victorian concoction that looked like a wedding cake. "Most of the houses date from the early 1800s, but a few are more recent, constructed to look as if they belong."

She must sound like an idiot, talking about architecture, but it was better than talking about why they were here.

"Let me guess," he said. "Yours was the real thing."

"Not ours." She thought of that cold excuse for a home. "It was always our father's house, not ours."

"Even so." Seth's voice held an odd note. "Lisa never gave me a clue that she came from a life like this."

"She wanted to forget it." Did you want to forget me, too, Lisa?

"It's a far cry from what she had with me."

Now she understood what that tone was in his voice. He was imagining that Lisa had compared what he gave her unfavorably with what she'd had here. She had to make him understand that wasn't so.

"There's a passage of scripture that says something like, 'Better a meal of herbs where love is than a banquet filled with envy and malice.' Believe me, Lisa cherished what she had with you." Her heart clenched, and she struggled to keep her voice even. "With you, Lisa was loved. That isn't just something. It's everything."

"I wish—" He shook his head. "I wish I'd pushed her more to tell me about her past. Maybe if I had—"

"Don't." She interrupted him sharply, and he glanced toward her in surprise at her tone. "You're letting yourself feel guilty for Lisa's death. Don't do that."

His fingers curled around the steering wheel. "I can't pretend about it, even to make myself feel better. Or make you feel better."

His words were like a separate little arrow in her heart. She fought to overcome the pain.

"We might both have failed Lisa, and we might spend the rest of our lives regretting what we did or didn't do. That's not my point now."

"What is?" His voice had hardened.

"My father has an innate ability to detect any weakness in the people he deals with. Including his children. If you let him sense your feelings of guilt, he'll use that against you. Believe me, I know."

Before he could respond, she leaned forward and pointed. "It's the next gate on the right. Just pull up far enough that the television camera can pick up your image."

Seth drew up to the gates, and in a moment they'd slid smoothly back. He drove through.

"State-of-the-art security."

"Yes. He lives a very well-protected life. Isolated, in fact. That's how he likes it."

Cold pain clenched her heart again at the thought of Davy living in that house. No. She wouldn't let that happen, whatever she had to do.

Seth drove up to the front of the house and parked at the edge of the curving drive. Instead of getting out immediately, he turned toward her, reaching across the seat to touch her shoulder lightly.

"What were you thinking about before? When you said that your father would use any weakness against you?"

She swallowed. "Too many instances to count them all."

"You were thinking of something specific, Julie." His hand pressed warmly against her shoulder. "I could hear it in your voice. Tell me."

"Are you trying to make up for the questions you didn't ask Lisa?"

"Maybe I've learned a little from that experience. Help me understand what put that pain in your voice."

She shrugged, embarrassed that she'd been so obvious. "I was remembering that incident I told you about. The college boyfriend who'd been ready to cash in on our relationship."

"Did you love him that much?" He touched her cheek gently.

Kindness, she told herself frantically. He's just being kind.

"Puppy love, I suppose. When my father told me about paying him off, he also made it clear to me that my 'ridiculous and obvious desire for love' had left me open to exploitation."

Seth drew in a breath, and she thought he censored several things he might have said. "That was brutal. You didn't believe him, did you?"

"Oh, yes. Because he was right. I *was* desperate for someone to love me."

"Julie—"

"No, listen. My pitiful little romance isn't important. And I eventually found that God's love more than made up for anything I'd been missing. What's important is that my father can find your weak spot and hit it. So don't walk in that door thinking about how you failed Lisa. Don't give him any ammunition."

He actually smiled. "Right, coach." He opened the door. "Shall we go into the lion's den?"

Her throat closed, and all she could do was nod. It was time.

* * *

So this was it. Seth took a deep breath as they walked toward the massive, double front door. He glanced at Julie. Her face was pale and set in the dim light.

"The last time I went into a mansion this big, it was a museum."

Her lips tightened. "A mausoleum would be a better description of this place."

Somehow that gave him confidence. Lisa had preferred a two-bedroom townhouse with him to all of this. He'd hold onto that thought and forget the rest.

Father, if I failed Lisa, I guess it's too late to ask her forgiveness, so I'm asking Yours. Forgive my failures and help me to do the right thing now.

They reached the door. Julie stopped. He'd have expected her to walk right into her father's house, but apparently that wasn't how the Alexanders did things. He tried to smile.

"It *is* like going into the lion's den."

She nodded. The look in her eyes told him she was afraid, but she wouldn't back down. She'd go with him all the way.

All of a sudden he felt the way he did when one of his brothers backed him up going into a fire. He couldn't have a better partner.

The thought startled him, but before he could explore it further, Julie lifted the knocker and let it fall. The door opened instantly, as if someone had been standing on the other side, waiting for them.

The middle-aged woman wore a gray dress that looked vaguely like a uniform. A housekeeper or secretary, he supposed. She looked at them without expression.

"Mr. Alexander is waiting in the study." She whisked away, disappearing through a doorway to the side of the huge hallway as if to disavow any relationship with them.

"This way," Julie murmured. Their steps clicked on the cold marble floor.

Her face seemed frozen, and he longed to bring it back to life again. Nobody should look that way at the thought of confronting her own father.

He nodded toward the carved oak door ahead of them. "His inner sanctum, is it?"

"He always called us there when we'd done something wrong. I think he draws strength from all the pictures on the walls. Don't let that intimidate you." Her voice was soft but determined.

Pictures? Before he could ask what she meant, they'd reached the door and she knocked. He grasped her other hand and squeezed it quickly, then dropped it. He couldn't let Ronald Alexander know he had feelings for Julie.

For just an instant he felt confused. He'd convinced himself he didn't have feelings for her, hadn't he? Maybe he hadn't succeeded.

A voice sounded from inside, and Julie opened the door. They'd only taken a couple of steps on the plush Oriental carpet when he saw what Julie meant about the pictures. The walls were lined with photographs of Ronald Alexander with virtually every powerful figure of the century.

Don't let that intimidate you, Julie had said. He forced himself to ignore the photos and concentrate on the man who sat behind the massive desk.

Gray. Everything about the man was gray, from his suit to his hair to his face. Even his eyes were gray. He was so still that he barely looked alive.

Something kept Seth still as Alexander's gray eyes shifted from him to Julie.

"Julia." His voice was flat. "I see that you've disappointed me. As usual."

"It's the other way around, Father." Her face was very pale, and Seth's heart ached at how vulnerable she was. "You lied to me."

Alexander dismissed her words with a wave of his hand. "I'm doing what is necessary. Don't take sides against me. You ought to know that's one thing I'll never forgive."

If it was possible for Julie to go any paler, she did. "That decision is up to you." Her voice was very controlled. "I've already made my decision."

Her father lifted his eyebrows. "How very enterprising of you. Surely you don't imagine that your support will make a difference?"

The contempt in his voice must cut her to the bone. How could a child possibly grow in an atmosphere like this?

"Your quarrel isn't with Julie." Seth took a step toward the man, longing to push Julie behind him, as if that would protect her from the power of her father's dislike. "It's with me."

Alexander's gaze shifted to him, and Seth understood what Julie had meant about being looked at as if one were a piece of defective merchandise. But he wasn't Alexander's child, and the man's opinion didn't have the power to hurt him the way it hurt her.

"I'm sure your attorney, if you have one, would advise you that coming here is a bad move."

"My attorney works for me. I wanted to see you for myself."

"And now you have." Alexander rose. "We have nothing to say to each other. Julie will show you the way out."

"I've got something to say to you." He stood his ground, knowing instinctively that it would be a mistake to retreat. Sometimes a man just had to stand and fight. "I don't know why you think you want my son, but you'll never get him. Ever."

Alexander smiled thinly. "You may be surprised by the power of money and position, Flanagan."

"Why?" The word burst from Julie. "Why on earth are you doing this? You can't be a father to Davy."

"Why?" For the first time some animation showed in Alexander's face. "You ought to know the answer to that. I've built a huge financial empire, and for whom? Both my daughters were weak, spineless creatures, just like their mothers. I should have had a son." His voice rose. "I deserved a son."

* * *

Julie absorbed the words, faintly surprised that they didn't hurt more. She'd always known what her father thought of her, so it didn't come as any surprise to have his dislike spelled out.

For God so loved the world—

The words resounded in her heart. She was loved. The thought gave her strength. She leaned forward, looking at him as if for the first time. Seeing him as he really was, instead of the way her childhood's imagination had painted him.

"We didn't deserve to be treated that way, Lisa and I. We'd have loved you if you'd ever given us a chance."

He raised his brows. "I don't want love. I want a son to mold into my image. To inherit everything I've built."

"Not my son," Seth said, steel in his voice. "He doesn't need anything you have to offer, and no court in the world would say you'd make a good father to him."

"Perhaps not. But I can make your lives miserable until I get what I want."

"You don't have any power over us."

Seth stood there, sturdy and strong, confronting her father. His good heart gave him a shield, but she feared it wouldn't be enough, not against a man like her father. She could see, so clearly, the difference between them.

"I have all the power." Her father's gesture took in

the photographs on the wall behind him. "That's who I am. You're no one. You can't win against me."

Her father's pride was exemplified by all those pictures of him with wealthy, powerful people. That was who he was—the man he saw in their eyes.

Seth was the man she'd seen through her camera lens—the caring friend, the loving father, the fearless firefighter. The honorable man.

He's everything a parent should be, Lord. He's everything that is meant by the word father.

Her heart clenched. She never referred to God as Father. She'd never been able to. Now she saw why.

Father. Her heart savored the word. *Show me, Father. Show me how to win this battle in Your name.*

Strength swept through her, slowly at first, then building into a healing flood. It chased out the fear and warmed her soul.

She could fight him. And she could win. She knew exactly what weapon to use.

"Stop it." She interrupted her father in the middle of saying just how he'd make Seth's life miserable. "You won't do anything to the Flanagans. You'll back away and leave them alone. I won't allow you to ruin Davy's life with your skewed values."

He shifted that cold gaze to her. "You won't allow? What do you imagine you can do? You have no power over me."

Her father's voice had its usual sneer when he spoke to her, but it couldn't hurt her. Not now.

"Actually, my power is only a mouse click away. If

you don't cooperate, I'll tell the whole world just who
the great Ronald Alexander really is."

"No one is interested in what you have to say."

"Believe it or not, Father, I'm a respected journal-
ist." She could almost smile. "And, as you've always
reminded me, what I do or say reflects on you."

"You won't find a publication to print such drivel."
For the first time, she detected a trace of uncertainty
in his voice.

"On the contrary, *Baltimore Living* would be happy
to run the piece I have in mind. If you'd bothered to
keep up with my career, you'd know that they often
run my articles. And the editor loves nothing so much
as showing the clay feet on public idols."

"I will not be blackmailed." But he took a step back.

"No? Then you'll find everyone you know laughing behind your back at the personal life of the great
Ronald Alexander—a man whose wives ran away
from him and whose daughters would do anything to
stay out of his grip."

"Do you think that matters to the people I know?"
He tried to maintain his facade, but she'd seen behind
it. She understood the one place he was vulnerable.

"Maybe not, but it matters to you. You're a sick, pitiful, weak old man, and by the time I'm finished, you
won't be asked to serve on the board of the trash authority." She waved her hand at the wall of photographs.
"Take a good look at them, Father. All of your rich and
powerful friends. And picture all of them laughing at
you."

For a moment longer he glared at her. She saw the exact moment when he recognized that she meant it—when he weighed her threat in the balance and decided that controlling Davy wasn't worth sacrificing the world's view of him.

"Very well," he said. "Get out and don't come back. You won't hear anything more from me ever again, either of you. Don't expect that I'll leave anything to you or to that child of Lisa's. I'll give it all to charity before I let you have a cent of it."

"We don't want it or need it." Did Seth realize they'd won? She didn't dare take her eyes off her father, as if to do so might relinquish control. "But I will take a notarized statement from you, saying that you give up all claim to Lisa's child. Seth's attorney will draw it up and send it over."

"Agreed." Hatred burned in his eyes, but it couldn't hurt her any longer. "Get out."

She turned toward the door, feeling Seth beside her. She was leaving, and she never had to come back. She was free of him at last.

Chapter Sixteen

The Flanagans were having a party. Seth supposed he shouldn't be surprised that his parents had greeted their return as a cause for celebration. The family milled through the house, laughing, talking, eating. Hugging each other. Praising God. A danger to one of them was a danger to all of them, and now that danger had been neutralized.

He hoped. He glanced around for Julie, to find that she'd backed herself into a corner. The expression on her face told him so clearly that she couldn't quite believe they'd all forgiven her.

He worked his way over to her. They hadn't talked much on the way back from Baltimore. She'd been exhausted, falling asleep in the car halfway home. Emotional exhaustion, he supposed. And even when she was awake, he hadn't quite been able to figure out what to say to her.

You saved us. That part was easy. It was the rest he hadn't figured out yet.

"Hi." He leaned against the wall next to her, studying her face. "You look wiped out."

"Just tired." She managed a smile, but her eyes evaded his.

"You're not afraid your father won't keep his word, are you?"

"No, definitely not. The attorney tied it up as airtight as possible. With that documentation, you could probably sue my father for harassment if he so much as looked cross-eyed at you."

"What's wrong, then?" He waved his hand at the family. "You're a hero. You should be celebrating. You saved us."

She shook her head. "You were doing a fine job of standing up to him on your own."

"Maybe, but I didn't know what his weak spot was. You did, and you used it brilliantly."

A shadow crossed her face. "I hate to think that means I'm like him."

"You're nothing like him." He put all the force of his conviction into his voice. Julie had to be sure of this. "You have a strong, analytical mind, and you finally found a way to defend yourself with it."

"I stopped thinking of him as all-powerful, that's all."

"You picked the right time to decide that."

A look almost of wonder came into her eyes. "I can only say that God was listening to my prayers. I finally saw what He's been trying to teach me for a long time—that as long as I was afraid of my father, I gave him power over me."

"I'm glad." He took her hand, wrapping his fingers around hers securely. "I hope you've stopped measuring yourself by his standards. He wasn't much of a father."

"No, he wasn't." She looked up at him then, and her eyes were so clear and deep he felt as if he were drowning in them. "When I saw what kind of a father you are to Davy, I knew what Lisa and I had wasn't even worthy of the same name."

He smoothed his fingers along the back of her hand, knowing he had more to say and not sure how to do it.

"You and Lisa were both hurt by him. If you're still thinking that you somehow failed Lisa, you ought to get rid of that burden. You weren't the one who failed. He was."

"I should have tried harder to stay in touch with her when she left. I should have made it clear that I was on her side, not his."

"Julie, you did the best you could at the time." He had to get this right. "I did, too. I know that now. Our best wasn't enough to counteract the doubts about herself that he'd planted in Lisa's heart, but we can't go on blaming ourselves for that. Lisa wouldn't want that."

"No, I'm sure she wouldn't." Julie glanced down, as if she were distancing herself from him. "She'd want you to continue being the best father you can to Davy. That's all she'd expect from you."

Something about her tone shook him. Was she trying to walk away from him? From Davy?

"And what about you?"

"I hope she'd want me to be a good aunt to her son." She glanced across the room to where Davy was building a tower of blocks with his cousin, unaware that all this celebration was on his account. "I hope you'll allow that."

"Allow it? If you try and walk out of his life now, I'll tackle you. We all will." A wave almost of panic swept through him. "You're not thinking of going away?"

She shrugged. "I have to go sometime. Maybe it would be best if I left for a while. I could come back for a visit in a month or so. Maybe sometime you'd let Davy come and stay with me."

"You can't go just like that. You're a part of Davy's life now. You can't go."

Julie carefully didn't look at Seth, because if he saw her face, he might see just how much she wanted to stay, to be a part of Davy's life. And of his life.

But he hadn't asked her for anything more. He hadn't mentioned any possible role for her but that of Davy's aunt. So she ought to get out as gracefully as possible.

"I do have a career. Maybe it's time I got back to it and let things settle down to normal here."

"You—" Seth frowned, and his fingers tightened on hers. "Your job—you could do it anywhere, right? You don't have to be in Baltimore all the time."

"No, but—" It's all I have.

No, she didn't want to say that to him. She didn't want to sound as if she was asking for his pity.

"You could stay here. Be a real part of Davy's life. See him every day."

And if she did that, she'd break her heart with loving Seth.

"I don't think so." She turned away, trying to blink back the tears that kept filling her eyes.

"Why not?" He grasped her shoulders suddenly, forcing her to look at him.

What she saw startled her. This wasn't the calm, easygoing man who was everyone's friend. This was a man filled with passion—a man ready to fight for what he wanted.

"I can't lose you." He said the words distinctly, as if determined that she understand exactly what he meant. "I can't let you walk away from us, Julie. I want us to be a family."

Her heart seemed to stop beating. She forced herself to look at him steadily. He hadn't said the most important thing, and she had to have the courage to ask.

"Are you still looking for someone who'll marry you for companionship, so you can give Davy a nice, safe mother?"

"You know that's not what I mean." His grip tightened, as if he'd hold her until she understood. "I never expected to love anyone again. That's why I thought I was willing to settle for less."

"And now?" It came out in a whisper.

"Now I want the whole thing. I want you. I love you, Julie."

Her heart was beating so fast it felt as if it would fly out of her chest. She couldn't possibly speak.

He touched her face, stroking her skin as if they were the only people in the room. "Tell me you love me, Julie."

For once, she didn't want to hide, even though she knew at least half the Flanagans had figured out what was going on by now and were watching them with bright, interested gazes.

"I love you," she said softly. "I love you, Seth Flanagan." She wasn't afraid to say the words. Her heart was open now, and all the fear was gone.

For God has not given us a spirit of fear, but of power, and of love, and of a sound mind.

Seth's smile broke through, and he drew her into his arms. Davy, apparently realizing something was going on, ran across the room to launch himself at their legs.

"Julie, hug me, too," he demanded.

Laughing, Seth lifted him into their arms, so that the three of them were entangled in an embrace.

A family. She felt their arms around her and knew this was true. They were a family. She'd longed all her life to have a real family, and now she did. She'd finally trusted all her fears to God, and He'd opened her heart to receive all He had to give her—love, abundant, overflowing love.

Dear Reader,

I'm so glad you decided to pick up this book, and I hope my story touches your heart. The Flanagan firefighter series is very dear to me, and I hope you enjoy reading about the firefighter heroes as much as I enjoy writing about them.

Julie and Seth both have burdens to carry, and I loved the fact that they could learn to share them with each other for the sake of a special little boy.

I owe special thanks to my daughter Lorie, for her photographic expertise, and to my grandson, Bjoern, for reminding me of what it's like to be three years old.

I hope you'll write and let me know how you liked this story. Address your letter to me at Steeple Hill Books, 233 Broadway, Suite 1001, New York, NY 10279, and I'll be happy to send you a signed bookplate or bookmark. You can visit me on the Web at www.martaperry.com or e-mail me at marta@martaperry.com.

Blessings,

Marta Perry

Take 2 inspirational love stories FREE!

PLUS get a FREE surprise gift!

Mail to Steeple Hill Reader Service™

In U.S.	In Canada
3010 Walden Ave.	P.O. Box 609
P.O. Box 1867	Fort Erie, Ontario
Buffalo, NY 14240-1867	L2A 5X3

YES! Please send me 2 free Love Inspired® novels and my free surprise gift. After receiving them, if I don't wish to receive anymore, I can return the shipping statement marked cancel. If I don't cancel, I will receive 4 brand-new novels every month, before they're available in stores! Bill me at the low price of $4.24 each in the U.S. and $4.74 each in Canada, plus 25¢ shipping and handling and applicable sales tax, if any*. That's the complete price and a savings of over 10% off the cover prices—quite a bargain! I understand that accepting the books and gift places me under no obligation ever to buy any books. I can always return a shipment and cancel at any time. Even if I never buy another book from Steeple Hill, the 2 free books and the surprise gift are mine to keep forever.

113 IDN DZ9M
313 IDN DZ9N

Name	(PLEASE PRINT)
Address	Apt. No.
City	State/Prov.	Zip/Postal Code

Not valid to current Love Inspired® subscribers.

Want to try two free books from another series?
Call 1-800-873-8635 or visit www.morefreebooks.com.

* Terms and prices are subject to change without notice. Sales tax applicable in New York. Canadian residents will be charged applicable provincial taxes and GST. All orders subject to approval. Offer limited to one per household.

® are registered trademarks owned and used by the trademark owner and or its licensee.

INTLI04R   ©2004 Steeple Hill

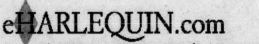